The Geranium Girls

# The Geranium Girls

## Alison Preston

*For Jacquie*

*Thanks so much for coming!*

*Alison Preston*

**Signature**
EDITIONS

© 2002, Alison Preston

Cover design by Terry Gallagher/Doowah Design.
Cover photo of Alison Preston by Tracey L. Sneesby.
Printed and bound in Canada by AGMV Marquis Imprimeur.

Thanks to Jan Beverage, Brenda Bourbonnais, Gail Bowen, Michael Bromilow, Eric Crone, Jacquie Crone, Steve Colley, Terri Colley, Adrienne Doole, Vic Ferrier, Susan Gifford, Kate Graham, Catherine Hunter, Lorraine Pronger, Reg Quinton, Cathy Small, Larry Small, Chris Thompson, and especially Karen Haughian and John Preston.

Thanks to the Manitoba Arts Council for its generous support during the writing of this book.

We acknowledge the support of The Canada Council for the Arts and the Manitoba Arts Council for our publishing program.

**National Library of Canada Cataloguing in Publication Data**

Preston, Alison, 1949-
     The geranium girls

ISBN 0-921833-83-0

     I. Title.

PS8581.R44G47 2002      C813'.54      C2002-901554-5
PR9199.3.P728G47 2002

Signature Editions, P.O. Box 206, RPO Corydon
Winnipeg, Manitoba, R3M 3S7

For Bruce

*Prologue*

Baby Frouten trudges the quarter mile from her home on the edge of town to the Texaco station on the highway. Sweat sluices between her fat thighs as she struggles against the white heat of the July afternoon.

She goes to see her friend, Hank the Bear—the burly man who owns the gas station. He lets her sit on a bench and watch him while he works. Hank is her only friend; he looks out for her, tries to keep the bad boys away. But she has had her share. Hank can't always be there.

Cramps start up in her belly, worse than the ones that come when she bleeds.

"May I use the biffy, Hank?"

"Of course, Baby. No need to ask."

It's more than an hour later when Hank rolls out from beneath Dick Wilson's nearly new '62 Ford and sees that Baby isn't there. He also sees the bright red spots on the cement and thinks for a second that they're petals. He follows them outside to the washroom at the side of the garage.

A dizziness comes over Hank. And he can't tell if the buzzing sound he hears is in his brain or if it comes from the flies lighting on the crimson pool that seeps out from under the door.

"Baby!" he shouts and tries the knob.

"Baby!" he roars and kicks the door down with one go.

No one knew; she was that fat under her cotton shifts.

Hank cuts the cord with his pocket knife.

"Hang on, Sweetheart." The words catch in his throat, unheard.

No one man could move Baby Frouten, not even Hank the Bear. He fears it may be too late to help her anyway. He wraps the tiny boy in a clean rag and phones the hospital to tell them what has happened. The closest ambulance is in Morden today—a good twenty minutes away. Hank careens through town in his pickup truck—drives to the hospital with one hand on the wheel. The small bundle rests quietly in the crook of his right arm.

On the way, he passes Doc Waters and the day orderly, Fred Briggs, in the doctor's car. They're on their way to tend to Baby at the gas station. Hank shouts out the window, "I'll be back to help in a minute, as soon as I drop this little tyke off."

Baby bleeds to death by the time they get to her.

A blessing, some say.

Baby's older sister, Hortense, is left to care for the newborn. The two women never knew their mother and their father had been killed eight months ago in an accident at the feed lot where he worked. Not that he would have been much good raising another kid. He wouldn't have won any prizes for the job he did on his own girls.

And as for the father of the infant, it could be anyone.

So Hortense brings up Baby's son. It's a job she wants. Maybe she can teach one boy some manners, teach him in such a way that he will know better than to hurt the likes of her sister who died.

And he could be used for other things. She can picture a few scenarios that look pretty good from where she stands.

Hortense keeps the boy on a short leash that she tugs too hard. She does more than that, but only away from the eyes of the town.

When she is busy in the house, she ties him to a chair, tightly, so he can barely move. When she is busy in the yard, she ties him to a tree, a shady spot where the mosquitoes have their way. If he cries she stuffs a wash cloth in his mouth till he simmers down.

One hot day, in 1966, Hank the Bear drives by the house and hears Hortense screaming louder than he believes possible. "Stop your whining," she screams. Hank feels it in his bones.

He stops the truck, unsure of what to do. He offers to take the boy to Rock Lake for the afternoon, for a swim and a romp.

"That would be fun, wouldn't it," Hortense says. Both the boy and Hank nod gingerly, afraid of the woman's voice echoing in their heads. Neither of them wanted to hear it again.

"Well, fun isn't what this child needs," Hortense says. But at least she says it quietly.

So no one interferes, not even Hank. No one wants to take it on.

Hank the Bear shudders the length of him the day he watches them board the bus for the city—the small boy in a harness and the tall thin woman, ramrod straight, who looks like she has a fishing rod poked up her ass.

When Hortense arrives in the city, one of the first things she does is buy a thin gold band at Woolworth's. She lets on that she's a widow; her husband died in a farm accident, she says.

With the ring on her finger, she changes her last name—goes to the Norquay Building, pays the basic fee of fifty dollars, and changes it to Keller. She can be whoever she wants to be. Hortense she keeps; she likes her first name, thinks it has a no-nonsense ring to it. There's very little nonsense about Hortense Frouten Keller.

She and the boy live in an apartment on Vaughan Street, across from the Bay, for a few years.

The Manitoba Telephone System hires her on as an operator. She hasn't done this type of work before but knows she will be good at it. Every morning, after dropping the boy off at kindergarten, and later, at school, she rides a bus to the telephone offices on Corydon Avenue. Hortense is a dependable employee; she takes her job seriously.

She saves up for a down payment on a house. It doesn't take long for them to move into a place of their own, as Hortense already has a nest egg from the sale of the old place in Pilot Mound.

# Chapter 1

It was a wet spring. The ground didn't get a chance to dry out between rainfalls. Beryl tramped through the bushes in St. Vital Park, away from the well-trodden paths. She slogged through long grass and thistles, poison ivy and mushrooms. Mushrooms in June! That's how wet it was. Her sneakers were soaked through.

Something long, solid and rounded, like a thin baseball bat, caught her hard in the arch of her foot. She lost her balance and toppled to a sitting position in the drenched forest. With one hand sunk in the boggy soil she boosted herself onto a fallen log where it wasn't quite so wet. Beryl removed her shoe and massaged the sore area. I should have stuck to the regular trail, she thought. I should be home drinking coffee.

"What the hell *was* that?" she muttered. Something stunk; she smelled her hand. And then her gaze drifted to the ground.

Her chest clenched. It squeezed and let go, squeezed again. A female form lay next to Beryl in the woods; she had touched it. It was the shin bone that had caused her to tumble to the ground. Bone on bone. No wonder it hurt so much.

Her breath didn't return for so long she thought she would die. She forced it. Manually—like turning off the toaster before it popped up the toast on its own—it could be done.

With her eyes she followed the long length of the girl—she was tall and very slender. Beryl hoped she was dead. Dealing with a live thing so close to death seemed beyond what she was capable of doing. She needn't have worried. This person was gone. Beryl knew this when she forced her gaze to rest upon the face. She had no experience with long-dead bodies, but no experience was necessary.

The dead girl's mouth was open wide. Mushrooms were growing there. Someone must have filled her mouth with dirt. How else could this be? Beryl closed her eyes for a long minute to give the face a chance to disappear. It didn't. A colony of mushrooms was using the head of a girl as a planter.

It rained softly at first, then hard, like a punishment.

She held out her hand and the rain washed it clean.

Pain in her foot. Pain from the shin bone of a dead girl. She could still feel the hard roundness pressing into her.

She wished she hadn't seen the face. The mushroom face. But she had; it was hers to keep. Like a birthmark, like a tattoo. Let me go back, she prayed, so I don't have to carry this forever.

## Chapter 2

The rain came lighter now.

Beryl snatched up her sock and shoe and stumbled through the trees in search of help.

The first people she met on the park road were an elderly man and woman in yellow rain slickers. She frightened them with her bare foot and stuttering explanations. Her teeth chattered as she spoke. It was the mushrooms that she mentioned.

"Sh...she has m...mushrooms in her mouth. Please help."

The man seemed willing to listen, but the woman dragged him away.

"Come on, Carl. She's obviously out of her mind on drugs or sniff."

"Sniff?" Carl asked. "What's sniff? Are you sure we shouldn't help her?"

"Yes, I'm sure! For goodness' sakes, come on!" the woman said. "She might have a knife or something."

Carl shuffled off at the end of his wife's arm.

"Sorry," he said.

"But she's dead," Beryl croaked and fell to her knees.

She didn't usually walk on a Saturday morning. It was a chance to stay home, sleep in. But today had been so crystal clear at the start, after the night rain. It enticed her and she hauled up her heavy one-speed bike from the basement. She pedalled through the glittering streets, turned in at the winding road leading into the park and locked her bike to a tree.

A tall man approached through the drizzle and crouched next to her on the road.

"Are you all right?" he asked, peering into her face. "Can I help?" His eyes were a deep blue.

She pointed to the spot in the bushes where the body lay, and said, "A dead girl... Please."

The man, who was very thin, like the girl, ploughed into the woods and out again.

"Dear God in heaven," he said.

"Then I...I didn't imagine her," Beryl said. She sat on the edge of the road, hugging her knees to her chest, oblivious to the wet.

"No. No, she's very real. Dear God."

The man fumbled through the pockets of his sweat pants for his phone and made the 911 call. The operator told him to stay on the line till the police arrived. She said it wouldn't be long. And they'd want his help to find the body.

"I'll be here," he said. "Don't worry. I'll wave them down. Joe. My name is Joe."

As Beryl and Joe waited for the cops to come the clouds shifted and the sun rose high in the June sky. They sat side by side on the edge of the road.

Lines from an old Lynyrd Skynyrd song played themselves over and over in Beryl's head: lines about the smell of death, the smell of death surrounding you.

A policewoman placed a small blanket around Beryl's shoulders, but she couldn't stop shaking.

"Let me help you with your shoe," Joe said and took a little blue towel from around his neck. It was damp but he dried her foot as best he could, removing old leaves and bits of twig. He fitted it back into the soggy runner, not bothering with her sock.

"I know it's probably not very comfortable," he said, "but you need to have shoes on."

"It's okay. It doesn't feel so bad."

They talked some, of small things. Joe Paine was a veterinarian out for a walk. He always walked in St. Vital Park on Saturday mornings, rain or shine. He had left his truck at the entrance, not far from Beryl's bike.

Mostly they just watched, quietly sitting, then standing, then sitting again in their damp spots by the side of the road, through the cordoning off of the area, through the photographer and the medical examiner, and all the other people who came and went, people whose jobs were connected to suspicious death. Finally they watched the careful carrying away of the long form of the mushroom girl.

Joe stayed a little too close at times. Beryl wanted people around, but she also needed to breathe. At one point, she couldn't tell if she was still shaking or if it was Joe's shivery presence beside her. And he smelled funny. Medicinal. Or maybe it was the inside of her own nostrils. Everything seemed very confusing.

Beryl heard a young cop call the girl "it."

"Looks like it's been here for a while," he said.

She wanted to object, but couldn't speak. Another policeman did it for her.

"Not 'it,' asshole," he said. "She!"

"Sorry, sir. I wasn't thinking."

The older cop wore street clothes, jeans and a golf shirt. He walked away, slowing by Beryl to say, "I'm sorry you had to see her."

He looked familiar.

"Thanks," she said.

He didn't seem to recognize her and she knew they'd never met, but she'd seen him before, she knew she had. He was from her neighbourhood; that was it. She was glad he was here now. His presence comforted her, more than that of the jittery veterinarian who had come to her aid.

Beryl wondered aloud why Joe didn't have any animals with him on his outing, his being a vet and all.

His eyes filled up.

"I've just been to the vet myself, actually," he said. "I had to have my old cat put down this morning."

"Oh, no," Beryl said. "I'm really sorry."

She reached out and suddenly didn't know where to touch him. She chose his forearm and used her good hand, which was the way she came to think of the hand that hadn't touched the girl.

"Jesus, I know how hard that is."

"Yeah. He was a wonderful cat. I had him since he was five weeks old. And he turned twenty last Tuesday. His name was Rollo."

Beryl took her hand back. "That's a good old age."

She said the words, but her heart wasn't in this. She wanted to be away from this man, to go home and shower and then bathe in fragrant bubbles and curl up in her nightgown in front of a wood fire and stare into it. If only it were winter. She looked over at Joe.

He rested his arms on his knees and his head on his arms.

"I think I may have jumped the gun," he said. His voice had gone wobbly. "I don't want to have done it today. Next week or next month, maybe, even tomorrow. Just not today."

"I'm sure you did the right thing. I know you did." Beryl moved away a little, wondering for a second if this was an act on his part.

How cynical is that, she thought.

The young cop, the one who called the girl "it," drove Beryl home. There was a general agreement that she shouldn't ride her bike. He settled it in the back of his van and drove her right to the door.

They didn't talk together at all. He tried a bit, words about the dampness and the mosquitoes, but he was too loud and Beryl couldn't answer. She didn't like his way of doing things.

"Thanks for the ride," she managed. And the mushroom face flashed behind her eyes.

# Chapter 3

The next day Beryl rode her bike to the St. Boniface police station to give a statement. Joe had offered to drive her but she needed to go alone. She wanted things to settle inside her and arrange themselves in ways she could see clearly. And she wasn't sure she wanted to see Joe again. How could she ever see him in any normal, undeathly sort of way?

Plus, he had been too insistent about giving her a ride. As though she couldn't possibly mean it when she said no thanks. She hadn't liked that. If there was anyone she would have wanted to accompany her today, it would be her dad, but he had been dead for fourteen years. She could have used his quiet strength now and she tried to feel it herself, as she waited for someone to come for her. But she couldn't manage it.

Yesterday's policeman, Sergeant Christie, called Beryl's name and guided her through a maze of cubicles. A picture of the mushroom girl was tacked to a bulletin board behind his desk—a picture of her face with her mouth open wide. Screaming wide. The photo was one of many items on the board, but it was the only one that Beryl saw.

She had been hoping for a different cop today. Sergeant Christie was civil enough to Beryl, but she didn't like him much. His pale eyes bored into hers and made her uncomfortable. She wondered if they taught that at policeman school.

He left her alone to write what she had seen on a pad of lined yellow paper. As soon as he was gone she slipped behind his desk and removed the photograph of the girl. She placed it in her backpack, careful to lay it flat, so it wouldn't get scrunched up amongst her other stuff.

An old banana rested at the bottom of her bag. She took it out and dropped it with a thud into Sergeant Christie's waste basket. It was the only piece of garbage in the metal container and in its advanced state it split open. Beryl dug deep into a side pocket and found an unopened packet of Kleenex, which she cracked.

She laid four tissues over the dead banana and said, "That'll have to do."

"What's that, Ms. Kyte?" It was the cop, Christie, back with coffee. "What'll have to do?"

Beryl hovered over the waste basket. She stood first on one foot and then the other. The empty pad of yellow paper glared up at them from the desk.

"I made a little mess in your garbage can. I haven't gotten started on my statement yet."

"What kind of a mess?" Christie's jaw tightened.

"Don't worry." Beryl suspected he thought she had vomited. "It's just a banana," she said. "An oldish one, I'm afraid."

"I see."

He disapproves of me, Beryl thought, and wondered why. Maybe he disapproved of a lot of things. Or maybe just her.

If only she had been assigned a nicer policeman, like the one who apologized to her in the park, the familiar one. Perhaps he was a boss and didn't have to work very hard.

The photograph in her rucksack was making her nervous. Maybe taking it had been a bad idea. She wished the cop would leave so she could think clearly and get on with her statement.

"I brought coffee," he said. "I was thinking you'd be almost done by now."

He placed the tray with its packets of sugar and non-dairy whitener on his desk beside the empty pad.

"Do you think you could get started on this, Ms. Kyte?"

If her dad were here, the sergeant wouldn't have such an attitude. Her dad had commanded respect without even trying. How had he done that?

Sergeant Christie joined her beside the waste basket and looked into it with her. The banana had soaked through the Kleenexes and permeated the room with its scent. He picked up the container and left the cubicle.

Beryl struggled over whether or not to talk about the mushrooms in her statement and decided against it. It seemed too private, no one's business but the girl's. And the killer's, of course. Definitely his business. She wondered if he had filled her mouth with dirt when he killed her; it seemed unlikely that it had happened on its own.

Suddenly she was alarmed at having taken the picture and wondered if she could fasten it back onto the bulletin board without getting caught.

Christie returned with the empty basket and sat down behind his desk.

"Sergeant?"

"Yes?"

"How did the woman die?"

"We're suspecting foul play at this time."

"Yes, I guess I kind of assumed that."

Beryl drew a little picture of a mouse next to her words on the page in front of her.

"I was just wondering," she said, "if you could tell me how it came about."

"No, I can't."

Beryl sketched in some long whiskers. "Does that mean you don't know, or that you just aren't going to tell the likes of me?"

Sergeant Christie smiled, but didn't speak. At least, Beryl assumed it was a smile; it wasn't a very good one, just a pursing of the lips. She decided she wouldn't want to kiss this policeman, under any circumstances. Not that it would ever come up. She suspected that he wouldn't want to kiss her, either. He probably thought she wasn't pretty enough to kiss.

"I see," she said. "I just have to wait and find out from the newspaper like everybody else? No special treatment for the finders of dead people?"

"No." His pinched smile was gone.

She finished her statement and signed it, scribbling out the little mouse before pushing the paper across the desk. She hadn't meant to draw it.

The photo was hers to keep. It reminded her of another photograph. When she had lived in Vancouver in the late eighties, the *North Shore News* had run a picture of a young native girl. Dead. It was an attempt to identify her, but it seemed wrong to Beryl. She had never seen such a thing before and she wondered at the legalities of it. If it was legal, why didn't it happen all the time? Maybe because it was wrong, even if it wasn't against the law.

No one had come forward to claim that girl. Not as far as Beryl knew anyway. She had cut that picture out and stared at it. The way she was going to stare at this one. The Vancouver girl's eyes and mouth had been closed at least, and she'd looked pretty in death.

Beryl didn't want to die in a way that would mean people snapping pictures of her and posting them on bulletin boards. She didn't feel as though photographs did her much credit when she was alive. It was doubtful she'd look any better dead. She supposed it was necessary, all this splattering about of dead faces, but it didn't sit well with her.

When she got home, Beryl gently removed the photo from her backpack and placed it in a drawer in her kitchen desk. She didn't feel up to looking at it again today.

She shook the rest of the contents of her bag out onto the kitchen table. There was a small stuffed animal, a chicken. Beryl had bought it for a guy at work whose wife had had a baby. But then she struggled with whether or not to give it to him. Maybe it was too much. Maybe it was too little. And then time went by and it was definitely too late. So now it belonged to her: a small peach-coloured stuffed chicken. She placed it in one pile.

Many tiny pieces of paper with names and phone numbers and e-mail addresses began another one. Joe Paine and Sergeant Christie were in that pile. She removed the policeman's card and formed another pile for recycling. If she ever had to talk to another cop, she didn't want it to be him.

A package of Player's King Size Extra Light. Beryl tried to smoke on social occasions only—dangerous behaviour; she could make a social occasion out of practically anything. The smokes formed a fourth pile.

The phone rang. It was Joe. She didn't want to talk to him, so she let the message run: "Hello, Beryl. Joe Paine here. I was just wondering how you got along at the police station. Call me."

He left a number, the same one that was on the little piece of paper. His home number; it was Sunday.

Joe seemed okay; he wasn't unattractive, if a bit skinny. His blue eyes were prettier than Sergeant Christie's, that's for sure. But they seemed naked somehow. Maybe his eyelashes were blond or missing or something. If she ever saw him again she would make a point of checking that out.

Beryl thought about the way he moved to help her. The trouble was, he cried. She realized that the circumstances called for crying, called for wailing like a banshee, but still, she didn't entirely trust Joe's tears.

She picked up the slip of paper with his number on it and put it in the recycling pile along with the sergeant's card. She couldn't imagine ever wanting to dial that number.

The phone rang again. This time it was someone named Gregor. Beryl couldn't figure out who that was. He left a brisk message about calling him back and it wasn't till he had hung up that she realized it was the sergeant. Gregor Christie, the sergeant, phoning about the photograph, of course, though he hadn't mentioned it in his message. It hadn't taken him long to notice that it was gone. Perhaps he gazed upon it in his spare time.

Beryl placed her Bic lighter next to the pack of cigarettes, then picked them both up, went out to the front deck, and chose a shady spot for her chair.

It definitely wasn't a social occasion, but the circumstances were unusual and called out for a change in routine: just one smoke.

## Chapter 4

Joe Paine was something of a celebrity, but Beryl didn't know it until Stan told her. They were sitting outside at the Second Cup on Graham Avenue with their bulging mailbags next to them. Beryl Kyte and Stan Socz were letter carriers. This stop for coffee had become a ritual for them, as their routes began in the same section of downtown Winnipeg.

According to Stan, Joe wrote a column in a magazine for animal lovers; the column was called *Doggie Dog Days*. Stan subscribed to the magazine and sang Joe's praises.

"He's very well thought of in animal circles," he said.

"Don't you mean animal lovers' circles, Stan?"

"Well, both then. I take my guys to see him and they love him. The only trouble is, he's so busy because he's so well liked. I doubt if he's taking any new patients."

"We're quite happy with Dr. Swirsky," Beryl said. "Can we please not talk about Joe anymore? I'm trying to not think about Saturday."

The morning was hot and humid. Summer lay heavy on the downtown streets, its weight stilling the air. Sweat trickled down both their faces.

"We're going to perish out here today," Beryl said. "It must be thirty degrees already."

"Maybe you should have stayed home for a while," Stan said. "For today, at least; Mondays are so hard."

"And do what? I'd be sitting there alone, freaking my own self out in one way or another. Coming to work helps."

"Yeah, this job is a riot," Stan said.

"Well, once you get out of that hell-hole it's not so bad." Beryl nodded in the direction of the main post office. "And at least in there this morning I could forget about Saturday for a few minutes here and there. There's so much other stupid stuff going on all the time.

"I think too much on the street, though," she went on, picking Stan's cigarette up from the ashtray where it lay burning, setting it down again.

It could be a lonely job, delivering mail. Once you hit the streets, it was just "good mornings," maybe helping the odd tourist with directions, some small talk: "Cold enough for ya?" "Hot enough for ya?" "Got any cheques in there for me?"

Stan knew all about Joe's cat, Rollo.

"Dr. Paine's been writing about him for years," he said. "He's gotta be devastated by that cat's death."

"Yeah, he is, actually. I probably should have been nicer to him, but I thought he might be inventing it."

"Jesus, Beryl."

A senior citizen who had bright orange hair and was wearing a great deal of makeup approached their table. "So this is why we get our mail so late in the day. You spend all your time drinking coffee with your cohort."

Beryl recognized the woman from a seniors' residence on her route. She smiled. "Hi, Mrs. Wren. You caught me, I guess." She thought the old woman was kidding.

"I'm going to report what I've seen here today. Don't doubt that for a minute. The very idea! Lounging about in a coffee shop while I'm waiting for my phone bill. Next you'll all be going on strike again." She shuffled off.

"I'm entitled to a coffee break!" Beryl called after her. "Bitch," she said quietly.

"Ignore her," Stan said. "She's just jealous because she saw you sitting with such a handsome guy."

Beryl smiled. "It's time I got going, Stan." She began strapping herself into her bag. "I'll see you later."

"I've seen parachutes fastened on people less securely," Stan said.

Straps criss-crossed over Beryl's shoulders to even out the weight and another one secured the bag at her waist. She had a double bag on order, one with two pouches so she could divide her mail evenly on both sides of her body. She looked forward to its arrival.

"My body thanks me for my efforts, Stan. You'll be sorry one day you didn't behave more like me."

"Heaven forbid," Stan said, "that I should behave more like you." He stood up and slung his thirty-five pound bag over one shoulder. And lit another cigarette.

"Anyway, I'm not going to live long enough to be sorry." He grinned.

"Stan?"

"Yeah?"

"I wish I hadn't given him my phone number. He called twice yesterday. I don't want him to phone me anymore."

"Who?"

"Joe!"

Stan smiled. "Don't worry, Beryl. He's a veterinarian."

"What's that got to do with anything?"

Beryl watched him lope off towards The Bay, noticing the stoop of his shoulders for the first time. She was sure he was smaller than he used to be and she worried that what he said might be true, about not living long enough to be sorry. Please don't die, Stan. But she could imagine it happening; she could picture herself at his funeral.

He turned around just then, as if he knew she was looking and gave a little one-finger wave. Beryl wanted to run after him, hug him to her chest. But they didn't have a hugging-type relationship.

So she began the walk down Edmonton Street, fixed tightly and sensibly into her bag, like a parachutist.

# Chapter 5

Beryl was stung by a wasp on a Saturday in the middle of June, one week exactly after she tripped over the girl in St. Vital Park. The wasp bumbled its way between her sandal and her freshly bathed foot. A prick that could have been a pine needle or a tiny shard of glass, and then the long sting that could have been nothing else.

"Fuck!" she cried. "What is it with me and my feet!"

The last time she had been stung her foot had swelled up like a foot balloon. She had feared it would keep on till it exploded.

Sitting down where she stood, in the middle of the sidewalk on Taché Avenue, she removed her sandal and the crippled wasp fumbled away to certain death. Three golden drops of poison balanced on the tender flesh of Beryl's instep next to the white circle where the wasp had stuck the stinger in. He'd have been fighting for his life at that point, she knew. Or was it a she wasp? Was it only the females who stung, like mosquitoes? Beryl always felt slightly embarrassed when she heard scientific information like that, that cast the female of the species in an unpleasant light. As though she and female mosquitoes were part of a giant sisterhood whose sole purpose was to inflict discomfort. And pain, if wasps belonged.

Beryl figured the sight of three tiny globules of liquid pain was a good sign. They weren't inside her. She brushed them away and decided not to try to squeeze out the poison that had entered her foot. In the *Free Press* the other day there had been a wasp article that said that squeezing sometimes makes the sting worse.

She put her shoe back on and continued her walk to the drugstore: a good destination under the circumstances. One of the pharmacists would be sure to give her some good advice. They were a lot more forthcoming than they used to be. Maybe the handsome one with skin the colour of creamy coffee would be there. Beryl had admired him from a distance since the first time she saw him there, several months ago.

Her friend Hermione's shop was just across the road and Beryl had planned to visit her today, but that would have to wait.

The pain wavered a bit and after a few minutes settled a notch or two below the worst. Another good sign. Her foot was reddening for sure, but not growing bigger. She favoured it as she walked and worried about movement making it worse.

It was the handsome pharmacist who served her.

"I've been stung by a wasp," she told him. "I'm a bit nervous because the last time it happened my foot swelled up to seven times its normal size."

The pharmacist left his perch behind the counter and hurried around to her side.

"When were you stung?" he asked.

"Just a few minutes ago," Beryl said.

The pharmacist, whose name tag said "Dhani Tata" guided her—pushed her really—to a bench where an elderly couple sat waiting for their prescriptions.

"Excuse us!" he announced and edged Beryl onto the bench next to them. The pharmacist seemed unsure on his feet, but he fell purposefully to his knees in front of Beryl.

The old woman began struggling to her feet but Dhani encouraged the couple to stay put.

"Where were you stung?" he asked Beryl.

"On my foot again, the right one," she said, and showed him the spot.

He removed her sandal and placed it on the floor.

"I'd like to try something now, but only with your permission," he said.

"Yes? What?" Beryl asked. "What do you have in mind?"

"I'd like to suck the poison from your foot as best I can, to try to minimize the reaction that way. It sometimes works for snake bites so I think it might be worth a try," he explained.

"Well...if you think it's worth a try, by all means," Beryl said. "Are you sure you want to?" She looked at her foot.

"Yes, quite sure."

And then his mouth was on her instep drawing out the poison. He spit once onto the floor.

"Sorry for spitting," he said. "I'll clean it up after."

The elderly couple observed with interest. A few other people had gathered by now and they watched as the pharmacist fastened his lips once more onto the soft inside of Beryl's foot. He sucked hard for all he was worth and spit again.

"I can taste it!"

He sucked till he couldn't taste it anymore.

Beryl felt relaxed. She wanted to close her eyes against the small gaping group, and lie against the chest of this odd man who had so willingly taken her foot into his mouth.

He returned her foot to her.

"Thank you," she whispered.

"I hope it helps."

She held her foot up in front of her and liked what she saw. Beryl thought of her feet as her best feature, though she had learned to keep that point of pride to herself. When she was a teenager she had mentioned it to a boyfriend once and he had said, "Nobody has nice feet."

It had hurt her feelings, but hadn't stopped her from admiring her own feet. If she was having a bad day, one of those days when she hated her face and her life and all the things she had done, and more things that she hadn't done, her feet sometimes helped—just the sight of them.

"You have beautiful feet," Dhani said quietly, so no one but Beryl could hear.

"Thank you," she replied.

"The show's over, folks." He spoke loudly now and the crowd loosened up a bit. A disappointment to those who arrived too late to see what the excitement was about.

"It's still going to hurt." He helped Beryl to stand up. "But I'll bet it won't hurt as much. Come and sit behind the counter with me for a few minutes and we'll talk about pain."

She obeyed. She wanted very badly to talk about pain with this man. What could be better! She followed as he toddled along. He had a peculiar way of walking, a bit Chaplinesque, Beryl decided. He leaned backwards, as though to keep himself from falling forwards, but almost to the point of tipping from overcorrection.

"Careful," she felt like saying, but didn't.

She sat on a chair and Dhani sat across from her on a stool. Two other pharmacists or pharmacists' helpers bustled about behind the counter. They smiled at Beryl and didn't seem to think she was out of place. Perhaps Dhani made a habit of acts such as these.

"Okay, so pain?" Dhani said.

Beryl felt again the hard round bone of the mushroom girl pressing into the arch of her other foot, the left one. A duller, achier pain than the sharp sting of the wasp.

"I came to think of it differently," he said, "before I had my toes done."

Ah, Beryl thought. So there's something wrong with his feet.

"Yes," Dhani said and Beryl tried to figure out from the way her mouth felt if she had spoken aloud. No, she was sure she hadn't.

"I had rheumatoid arthritis in my toes," he went on. "It was so bad there was nothing to do but chop them off."

Beryl let out a little gasp.

Dhani held up one of his own feet.

"There are special slippers inside my shoes, with toes built in. False toes all in a clump. A malleable clump so it doesn't hurt my stumps.

"Anyway," he continued, "the business with my toes was the worst pain I ever had. Not so much after they were lopped off, but during the time leading up to the operation. Pain killers weren't very effective and, anyway, I didn't want to end up in Winnipeg's version of the Betty Ford Center."

He smiled at Beryl. "So I came to think of pain a little differently."

"I'm sorry about your toes," Beryl said. "You seem very young to have rheumatoid arthritis."

"Yes, I am young," Dhani said. "Just thirty-nine now and the operation was four years ago." He held up both shoes this time. "I'm still getting used to my new feet.

"Anyway, I decided to begin from scratch with the pain. Pretend I had just met it and treat it differently from the vantage point of this new start. It was a presence all right, one that couldn't be ignored. But it didn't have to be the boss like it seemed to have been for so long.

"I didn't call it pain anymore. I called it Roberta. Roberta was my powerful companion. I felt her presence but it wasn't unpleasant anymore. It simply was."

Beryl wanted to ask why he gave the pain a woman's name. Was all pain part of the same sisterhood that she and mosquitoes and maybe wasps belonged to? But she let him go on.

"Roberta came and went as she always had. I started to miss her a little when she vanished completely and I greeted her heartily when she returned. She became a bit like a big unwieldy dog who's more trouble than she's worth but whom you love to pieces."

"You loved your pain to pieces?" Beryl asked.

Her foot began to throb and she wanted to raise it and rest it on a pillow, or on Dhani's knee. She wanted to sleep. The talk of his relationship with pain was all very well, but she knew she wasn't the type of person who could pull off something like that.

"I'm sure I wouldn't have the patience," she said. "I'd succumb, like I'm succumbing now."

Dhani leapt up.

"I'm sorry," he said and lurched over to a small freezer where he reached in and came back with a cold pack. He wrapped it in a towel and pressed it to the sting and then sat down again with her foot upon his knee.

"The ice should help and I'll give you a couple of Tylenols before you go."

"Is it the female of the species, do you know," Beryl asked, "the female wasp that does the stinging?"

"I don't know," Dhani said.

She longed to talk to him about the thing that had happened to her left foot last Saturday, the other thing she'd stepped on. She would tell him, but not just now. For sure she would be seeing him again.

He was thirty-nine. Was that too old for her? She was just twenty-nine last November. Ten years difference. When she was fifty-nine, he'd be sixty-nine. When she was eighty-nine, he'd be ninety-nine. Georges had been older too, but not by so much. That hadn't turned out very well. But he was nothing like Dhani.

"Call me later and let me know how your foot is," Dhani said as she was leaving. "I'm here till nine."

On her way home Beryl realized she had forgotten to pick up the shampoo that she had been heading to the drugstore for in the first place. The coupon was folded inside the pocket of her shorts.

Certain things inside her had begun changing since last Saturday. She couldn't describe the changes or even be absolutely sure what they were, just that they were there. Or maybe the whole of her was shifting, not just things inside her. She didn't know.

And she was missing her dad for the first time in her life. She hadn't even particularly liked him when he was alive, but now she wished she could ask him things and apologize for being the way she was.

Plus, she was doing things she'd never done before, like cutting out coupons, for one: she'd never done that. And washing her hair twice a day. That's why she needed more shampoo. She was counting on getting over that one. It was too much.

Please, don't let there be a message from Joe, Beryl prayed, as she unlocked the door and stuck her key back under the flower pot. He had phoned every day for the past week and she didn't want to talk to him. She was never friendly and was starting to be rather short with him. She wanted to shout: "Can't the most popular man in the pet world find someone who actually wants to talk to him?" But she didn't.

There was no message from Joe. But there was a hang-up. Beryl dialed *69 to see if she could find out who it was, but the taped voice started with the "We're sorry" business.

Maybe Joe was starting to get that he was bothering her.

Beryl phoned Hermione to let her know she wouldn't be by today and why.

"No problemo," said her friend. "Put your foot up and relax."

Beryl put on her favourite Little Feat disc, the one with "Willin'" on it, the live version, and lay down on the couch to rest her foot. Her two cats, Dusty and Jude, joined her there. She drifted off, with Lowell George's voice, singing—telling her how he'd driven every kind of rig that'd ever been made, how he'd driven down the back roads so he wouldn't get weighed.

*Chapter 6*

The part he liked best was filling her mouth with dirt. He was surprised that it was hard to keep open. It wanted to shut itself against his efforts. He had to pack it full. Her mouth wouldn't open and her eyes wouldn't close. She watched him all the while. He would have preferred that she didn't, but in a way it was better. It stirred him; his body told him so.

His hand reaches now for his glass of water. The thirst never goes away; he hates his thirst. Without taking even a sip he hurls the water down the drain.

He pictures the flower pots that used to line the window sill above the kitchen sink. The old wood frame house belonged to Aunt Hortense in those days. Or Auntie Cunt as he thought of her. Auntie Cunt and her geraniums.

How he hates the smell of geraniums! Heavy, oily, pungent stink. And then they change and smell like apricots. Tricky, nasty flowers. He hates apricots too.

She had needled him into helping her. Always with the dirt. Feel the dirt on your hands, Boyo. Don't be afraid of the dirt.

Boyo feared far more than dirt but he didn't let on. He smiled. Because she told him to. He smiled because if he didn't she tied his mouth open with one of her slippery woman scarves. She hadn't wanted any gloomy Guses in her house!

It was on one of those dirt days that Hortense finally told him something about his mother.

"Your ma was a 'tard, if you must know," she said.

"She was a what?'"

"A retardo. Dull as that lump of dirt in your hand, Boyo. Born that way."

He dropped the soil and ran.

If his own mother had been retarded, what hope was there for him? He did well enough at school, but Aunt Hort could not be satisfied. If he got a B, he was punished for not working hard enough; if he got an A, his mark was regarded with suspicion: he must have cheated; the teacher must be a moron.

His punishments were many. Much of the time he had no idea what he had done wrong. If he had, he would have gladly apologized, not that it would have helped.

The punishments usually took some form of denial. The worst one was when she wouldn't let him use the biffy, as she called it. She would see him walking towards the bathroom and shout, "Not so fast, Boyo! Where do you think you're going?"

"To the bathroom," he said.

"Let's just see if you can hold on a little longer," she said. "Are we talkin' number one or number two?"

"Both, I think."

"See if you can hold on till morning."

So he would try to go at school, when he was away from her, but often, to his huge frustration, he would sit and sit inside a cubicle in the boys' room but nothing would come out. More than once, he wet his pants in the classroom or in the gymnasium during physical education. He was tormented mercilessly by the other kids in the class. Stink Boy, they called him.

Sometimes, on his way home from school, he would go down to the river and seek out a little privacy there to do his business. One time Hort saw him coming up from the bushes lining the river bank and suspected him of doing just that. She got out the duct tape that time and covered the head of his shrivelled penis.

He wasn't allowed out all weekend. She kept him in the house where she could keep an eye on him and use him for what she called a scrub and rub.

Hortense's house belongs to him now—has for years. It came to him by default, as her closest living relative, her only one. She didn't leave a will. She hadn't expected to die.

He writes a name on the doodle pad they gave him for free at St. Leon Gardens, the market where he buys his fruit. Beryl Kyte, he writes. It's the name of the woman who found the tall one. He wonders what the person called Beryl is doing right now.

# Chapter 7

Beryl was watching her neighbours to the south, the Kruck-Boulbrias, heading out to their mini-van on Sunday morning. They had two squirrels in a cage.

They did it all the time—captured squirrels and drove them someplace.

"We live in a treed neighbourhood," she said, after saying good morning and not meaning it. She did not wish them a good morning. She wished them different personalities, that would allow them to leave the squirrels where they belonged.

"In these parts wherever there are trees there are bound to be squirrels," she went on, yanking weeds out of the garden along the fence where she had planted lettuce and carrots.

Mort, the husband, looked sheepish. "My wife is afraid of the squirrels," he said. "She hears them on the roof and they scare her."

They both did that—called each other "my wife" and "my husband" instead of using their actual names.

Ariadne, the wife, was already in the vehicle with the door closed and the window rolled up, looking straight ahead.

Beryl wanted to say, "Why don't the two of you move into a cement building surrounded by cement and leave the squirrels alone?"

But she didn't. She left it and went back to pulling out the little elm and maple seedlings that were trying to take root in her tiny vegetable garden.

Why am I so grumpy? she wondered. Why can't I be more like Stan, with his easygoing ways, his ability to laugh at stuff rather than throw fits about it? He'd probably be best friends with the Kruck-Boulbrias. He'd probably teach them to like squirrels.

The phone rang and she ran to listen to the message. She was hoping to hear from Dhani. They were planning an evening out.

It was Joe. He didn't give his usual spiel about how he thought she might want to talk, he knew he did, and so on. This message was short and to the point: "Hello, Beryl. Joe Paine here. I just wanted to let you know I won't be bothering you anymore. So, good luck, I guess, and that's about it. Okay, bye." It was obvious by the odd lilt at the end of his sentences that he was trying to keep the resentment out of his voice, but he didn't quite manage it.

An uneasiness crept in, only mildly tempered with relief. What had happened other than the fact that she had never been nice to him when he called? Maybe Stan had said something to him. She tried to recall if he'd said anything about having to take Scrug or Leo to the vet lately. She didn't think so, but couldn't be sure.

Beryl had been whining a lot to Stan about Joe but she hadn't actually wanted him to do anything about it. I should just keep my whining to myself, she thought, and talk to Stan about football and the post office. But both of those topics would probably involve whining too.

She wished she hadn't recycled Sergeant Christie's phone number. She hadn't returned his call and was mildly curious that he hadn't tried again.

Beryl wondered how the investigation was going, wondered if the cops would tell her anything if she phoned.

After the first flurry of stories in the *Free Press*, about the discovery of the body, there hadn't been much. Just a short paragraph a few days later, saying that the police were following up some leads, that the trail was by no means cold. That could mean something or absolutely nothing.

And they mentioned a hooker, Charise Rondeau, who had been murdered about a year and a half ago. Her killer had never been found. They hinted at a possible connection between the two deaths. Charise's body had been dumped in a parking lot off Higgins Avenue, close to the Low Track, on a bitterly cold winter night. There was no mention of how either woman had died.

Beryl's picture had been in the paper on that first Sunday. She'd been huddled under a blanket by the side of the road. They identified her as Beryl Kyte, the "jogger" who had tripped over the body. She wasn't a jogger; she never ran if she could help it. But at least her name had been spelled correctly.

The phone rang again and this time it was Hermione, so Beryl picked it up. Her friend just wanted to know how she was getting along. It had been awhile since they had seen each other face to face, although they had spoken on the phone several times since the events in the park. The two of them decided that Beryl would drop by the shop one day soon on her way home from work, so they could get properly caught up with each other.

# Chapter 8

Beryl and Stan sorted their mail side by side, with conveyor belts rumbling over their heads. The sound always caused Beryl to feel that she was wearing a hat that was far too tight. Something needed a lube job this morning. There was a terrible screech every few seconds.

"Have you been to the vet lately?" Beryl asked.

"What!"

"Have you taken either of your guys to the vet lately?" Beryl shouted above the cacophony.

"No. I've been there, but only to pick up Scrug's food. Why?"

"Did you say anything to Joe Paine about me?"

"Jesus! Me, me, me! Yeah, actually I did."

"I knew it. Damn! What did you say?"

"Let's go for a smoke."

"I don't smoke on weekday mornings."

"That's okay. You can watch me. We should get out of here for a few minutes anyway, before we do permanent damage to our ears."

"Okay, let's go."

They sat on a low pebbled wall across the street at the library. It was cool there in the shade of the downtown buildings, a relief from the sticky heat inside the post office.

"I wish you hadn't said anything to him, Stan. What did you say, anyway?"

"Nothing. I was just kidding. I didn't even see Joe. I just dealt with the folks out front. If I had seen him I probably would've said something, though. I mean, you've been going on and on and on about how much he's been driving you crazy with his phone calls."

"Wait a minute. You were kidding? You didn't say anything?" Beryl stood up and faced Stan.

"Yeah. No. Whatever. No. I didn't say anything."

"Jesus Christ, Stan! I should slap you." Beryl did give him a little shove but it didn't move him anywhere.

Stan inhaled deeply, letting a little smoke out first so it could travel up his nose.

"May I have one of those?" Beryl asked.

"No."

"Why are you being so mean to me this morning?" Beryl's voice shook a little. "Stan, you shouldn't tease me about stuff like Joe. It's not a good joke." She slumped back down beside him on the wall.

Stan gave her his second-last smoke and lit it.

"I'm sorry. The post office brings out the worst in me."

He left a message on my machine," Beryl said, "saying he wasn't going to bother me anymore. I feel kind of bad about it." She took a long drag on her cigarette. "Ah. God, that's good."

Stan took one last puff on his, right to the filter, and rubbed it out on the wall beside him.

"That's a good thing, isn't it?" he asked. "Him not bothering you anymore?"

"Well yeah, I guess. It's just that I don't want to have hurt his feelings. Or, what if he's insane and I've sort of set him off or something?"

"I don't think he's insane," Stan said. "I think he was probably genuinely worried about you and feeling weird himself about what the two of you saw in the park. Also, he may have a bit of a crush on you."

"How do you know he's not wacko? He's phoned me a wacky number of times."

"Because he's a successful veterinarian."

"So!"

"So animals wouldn't like him if he was insane in a dangerous way, I don't think. Do you?"

"No. I guess not. That's a good point. I wonder if any murderers get along well with animals. I wonder if Ted Bundy had any pets. He was a fairly personable killer."

"Are you actually thinking that Joe may have been involved in the girl's death?"

Beryl flicked her butt out onto the road and a transit bus drove over it.

"We better get back," she said. "No, I'm not thinking that, I guess. Jesus, I don't know what I'm thinking."

They crossed Smith Street, digging in their pockets for their identification cards, and entered the employees' entrance of the post office.

"I guess it was just my unresponsiveness and nastiness that made him decide not to bother me anymore," Beryl said, as they rode the escalators back up to the third floor.

"That'd likely do it," Stan said.

Their supervisor, Ed, was looking for both of them when they got back. He had a new bag for Beryl and a complaint for Stan. The complaint was from a woman who thought Stan was too rough with her mail. She had accused him of bending things that didn't need to be bent for what she had described as "the sheer joy of bending."

"The sheer joy of bending?" Stan said.

"That's what it says here," Ed said, waving a piece of paper. "I'm just telling you what the customer service people sent along to me."

"Oh, man." Stan heaved a sigh. "This place is gonna kill me."

Beryl fumbled around with her new double bag, fastening big buckles and little ones, trying to adjust the straps.

"I think this is a two-person job," she muttered. "How do people know how to do these things?"

Two of her fellow letter carriers, a man and a woman, stopped what they were doing and fastened Beryl into her new bag. They fussed and discussed and rearranged what she had already done till it was just right and she felt six years old and very cozy.

"Thank you," she said. "Thank you both." She was alarmed to find her eyes filling with tears.

Good Lord, not now, she prayed.

Her eyes filled up at the drop of a hat. This was something new for her too, along with cutting coupons and washing her hair too often. She supposed it would pass.

## Chapter 9

Dhani and Beryl stepped out the open door of Pasquale's Restaurant into the summer night. Cars whizzed by on Marion Street and they walked quickly till they reached the flood bowl and then the quiet street by the river that led to Beryl's house. The night was still, not a whisper of a breeze, and the mosquitoes were elsewhere, maybe in the scrubby vegetation near the water or bothering other people in their yards.

Beryl looked sideways at Dhani as they walked. She liked his appearance. He was strong looking and not thin. She didn't trust thin past a certain age. There was a steady look to his deep brown eyes.

They fell into step under the clear night sky. The stars were barely visible—too much light from the city.

Beryl carried a small box with most of a Neapolitan pizza inside. Dhani carried nothing. He left his entire sausage and mushroom pizza at the restaurant. They had eaten so many appetizers that they had been almost full before their main courses arrived. Beryl had been mildly ashamed at her own gluttony, if not Dhani's, but he had convinced her not to worry about it.

"We're celebrating," he had said. "And besides, we can take our leftovers home. We'll eat them. Nothing will be wasted."

But then his pizza had arrived and the mushrooms stared across the table at Beryl and she found herself blurting out a version of her experience in the park. Dhani knew about it, the murder, he had read the bits in the paper. But he hadn't known about Beryl's part in it. Her name was in the paper just the once, a week before they met. The conversation pretty much put an end to eating, but Dhani was such a kind and eager listener that Beryl felt good about sharing her story with him.

"I'm worried that I'll never be able to eat mushrooms again," she said, "and I used to really like them."

Dhani reached across the table for her hand. "I'm sorry I ordered mushrooms on my pizza," he said.

Beryl smiled. "It's okay. You didn't know."

"I really like tomatoes," she had gone on, "probably even more than before. They seem pure to me, friendly even."

"I love summer," Dhani said now as they strolled down Lyndale.

Beryl could feel his eyes on her bare arms and on the curve of her breasts beneath the pale blue cotton of her dress.

She laughed, a light sound.

"Why?" She had an inkling of what he was thinking but didn't think he would really say it.

Dhani gestured widely to take in the whole of Beryl and a little of the river park area—to safen it up a bit, she supposed.

At that moment, at the moment of Dhani's safe gesture, two cars screamed past them down the drive and screeched to a halt just a half-block away. Both drivers leapt from their vehicles. One shouted and the other stared in disbelief. It was as though he was caught up in a standoff against his will: the reckless chase and roadside confrontation had happened to him. He had let them, though, and now he was paying. The two men stood in the bright light from a street lamp and Beryl realized at once that the quiet one was the policeman from the neighbourhood, the one who had spoken to her in the park.

"You dumb fuck!" yelled the other man. "You could have caused an accident back there! If I wasn't such a skilled driver you would have, you careless prick!"

Beryl hoped for violence. More than just the shouting. Shouting was nothing, old hat. She didn't want to be a witness to nothing.

The policeman stared at the man, who was standing too close to him. He was in his face.

"Or maybe you're drunk, are you?" the man shouted, "keeping company with your piss-tank of a wife."

The policeman swung at the hollering man. Perhaps he felt like Beryl did about empty shouts. It was a solid punch and she and Dhani were near enough now to hear a bone crack. And to see the blood flow. It shut the man up for a moment. Then he called his attacker by name.

"Fuck me, Frank. You've broken my nose."

"They know each other," Beryl whispered to Dhani. They edged closer. Close enough to see the shoulders of the man who had thrown the punch. Frank's shoulders. Beryl placed him more particularly now, seeing him once more and hearing his name; he lived on Claremont. She had seen him with his kids on their bikes and in the flood bowl with their dog. The dog's name was Doris.

The punched man started yelling again. This time about suing and lawyers and dead meat.

Not a word from Frank.

Hit him again, thought Beryl. Hit him again.

Dhani moved to intervene and Beryl grabbed his arm. "No!"

Frank didn't hit him again, though. He got into his car and pulled away, slowing down to speak to the woman who sat immobile in the punched man's car.

"Sorry, Sylvie," he called. "Sorry about all this."

Sylvie looked straight ahead till Frank drove off. Beryl approached and leaned down to the open window on the driver's side. She could see from the look on Sylvie's face that she, too, was glad that Frank had thrown the punch.

"Are you all right?" Beryl asked, hearing the feebleness of her question, but not knowing what else to say.

"No," said Sylvie.

The man with the broken nose sat on the curb with his head back, swallowing blood.

Dhani crouched beside him and said, "I'm a pharmacist."

"Congratulations," said the man.

Dhani took a phone from his pocket.

"Please don't!" shouted Sylvie. "Please don't call anyone."

"Are you sure?" Beryl asked.

It didn't do any good, Dhani not calling for help. Someone else must have phoned the police because they were suddenly there, arguing with the injured man about going to the hospital. He didn't want to; he didn't even want to press charges. A sheepishness seemed to have taken him over.

Beryl and Dhani had to tell the police what they had seen.

Frank had spoken to Beryl on that day two weeks ago, the day of the mushroom girl. I'm sorry you had to see her, he'd said. She didn't want to say anything now that would get him into trouble.

So mostly she said, I don't know and I didn't really see much—things like that—while Dhani stared at her. For his part he answered truthfully and completely and it came out as though they were describing two different movies.

It seemed unbelievable to Beryl that she had to speak to the cops twice in so short a time. Some people must go through life giving no statements to the police. Or statements connected to break-ins or car thefts or mischievous kids. Not because twice in less than two weeks they were witness to something terrible.

When Dhani and Beryl were done they turned to Sylvie to see how she was getting along and saw that she had left, on foot. Beryl didn't blame her, wouldn't if she kept right on walking. It wouldn't take long to get your fill of someone like Menno Maersk. That was what the guy's name turned out to be.

"Women in dresses," Dhani said.

"What?"

"Women in summer dresses, like the one you're wearing. That's why I love it so much. Summer, I mean."

They sat drinking Lynchburg Lemonades at Muddy Waters' bar by the river; they were too wound up to go home. Dhani ordered a dessert, a huge brownie with ice cream and chocolate sauce.

The river was high, inches from the sidewalk. It was going to cover the walkway again, the paper had said, because of all the rain. Beryl was enjoying sitting here with Dhani, listening to him and wondering if they would have sex.

"It's one of the reasons, anyway," he said. "One of the big ones."

Pleasure nudged at Beryl, pleasure and bourbon. She smiled.

"Would you like a bite? Dhani asked.

"No, thanks." Beryl didn't think brownies went very well with Lynchburg Lemonade, but she kept that to herself.

She thought about Frank, the beleaguered policeman, and was glad he lived in her neighbourhood.

Dhani ate the ice cream but asked the waitress to package up the brownie for him.

"Why did you lie to the police tonight?" he asked Beryl.

"I didn't lie," she said. "I just pretended I didn't see much."

"Pretending is the same as lying when you're talking to cops."

"No, it's not."

"Yes, it is."

Beryl explained to Dhani that Frank was the policeman from the park, the one that had made her feel a wee bit better on that horrible occasion.

"He seems kind of hot-headed to be a policeman," Dhani said.

Beryl sighed. "I like Frank and I didn't like that Menno character at all," she said. "He was nasty and violent."

"And Frank wasn't?"

"No. That guy insulted Frank's wife. Didn't you hear him? What would you have Frank do? Nothing?" Beryl sipped her golden drink.

"Besides, the guy didn't want to press charges, anyway. Not everything has to go through official channels. It didn't matter what I said."

"Yes, it did," said Dhani.

Beryl felt some disappointment in Dhani.

"Also, Beryl…" Dhani was drinking through a straw. "Why did you stop me from intervening, when it looked as though Frank might hit Menno a second time?"

"I didn't stop you. You could easily have shaken me off."

"But why did you put your hand on my arm?"

"I don't know."

"And you said 'no.' Why did you say 'no'?"

"I don't know, Dhani. I guess I wanted it to run its natural course."

"Hmm."

"What do you mean, hmm?"

"Just hmm."

"That sounds like kind of a judgmental hmm to me," Beryl said.

"Well, it probably is," Dhani said, draining his glass. "Come on, let's walk you home." He picked up his brownie in its large Styrofoam container.

Beryl began to wish she hadn't confided in Dhani about the mushroom girl. She left her pizza at the bar on purpose. It was probably spoiled by now anyway.

They crossed the foot bridge and the Norwood Bridge and walked all the way down Lyndale Drive to Beryl's street without saying a word. Dhani threw his brownie into a public waste container on the drive.

"I'm sorry," he said, and Beryl didn't know if he was talking to her or the metal garbage can.

She wondered when they parted at her door if she would ever see him again outside his capacity as a pharmacist.

But then he touched her cheek before he turned away and said, "What are you up to tomorrow?"

"I don't know," she said.

"Do you want to do something with me?"

"Yes," she said. "Yes, I do."

## Chapter 10

Beryl awoke, stunned that she could be capable of such violence, even in a dream. Why hadn't she stopped when the girl was beaten into unconsciousness and certain death? Why had she kept on? Her stomach heaved and she sat up.

Sweat bathed her naked body and she shivered in the light breeze from the open window.

*In the dream she sees the options before her, not to start on the girl or to deal with her differently—with words maybe—or silence. Or at least to stop sooner and save herself from having to live with what she is doing. She sees the progression as she connects with that pale smooth face, over and over again, feels in her gut the bloody hell that she'll never be rid of. She is snuffing out her own life in a sense, with that stubby baseball bat. But she rages on. It is bigger than the part of her that says no.*

Only in dreams, thought Beryl. Whose face was that anyhow?

She put on her summer robe and went out into the warm night. She had the best deck east of the Red River. Smooth with good wide steps all around.

A siren soared down Main Street and Beryl's hands shook as she lit her cigarette.

The siren is not for me.

She inhaled deeply. The dream probably wouldn't have happened if it hadn't been for that business on Lyndale Drive with the man named Menno. And anyway, if she was perfectly honest with herself, she didn't completely hate the dream.

More sirens: they're not for me.

# Chapter 11

Fucking geraniums! He wants to avoid them. But they're always there when he walks down Taché: to the bank, to the barber, the shoemaker, any Christly place he goes. He decides to try a different route, maybe down back lanes, to get where he is going. Then he changes his mind. Why the fuck should he!

She even has them in hanging pots along the side stairs that lead up to what Boyo suspects is her apartment. At night when he walks by he sees those tiny white lights, like the ones that decorate the trees on Broadway. They wind up the stairs, light up the pots.

He thinks he can smell the geraniums at night. And it's always different. Just like the ones he used to work on with Auntie Cunt. Lemony sometimes, sometimes like nutmeg. That's why he hates eggnog so much. The thought of it makes him gag. They smell like pepper, too, at times. But worst of all is the rose scent; the sickly old-lady smell of roses.

Some of the geraniums are the colour of blood. His mother's blood.

"Your ma bled to death, if you must know," Aunt Hort said, "birthing you."

If you must know, she always said, as though it wasn't his business. He wished that it wasn't.

"If it weren't for you, she would probably still be alive," she said and grabbed his wrist and dragged him to the bathroom where he watched her as she bathed. And dreaded what came next.

Scrub and rub.

With Hort kneeling in the tub and Boyo kneeling outside of it, he bent over to her demands. He soaped up the wash cloth and scrubbed her clean. Down there. He rinsed and soaped again. Rinsed. Then came the worst part. With his bare fingers he rubbed her. She guided him with her movements and her own hand, till she lurched and shuddered and told him to stop.

"Did you enjoy that, Boyo?" she asked.

What could the right answer possibly be?

"No?" he tried.

Wrong. Duct tape on his tender parts. Not just the head of his penis this time.

"Did you like that, Boyo?" she asked on another occasion.

"Yes."

Wrong again. Standing perfectly still. Not moving. Not moving for hours. Or else.

An idea forms in his mind now: he could wreck the flowers. All of them! The hanging ones will be easy; they are fairly small. But he'll have to think about the big pots and the ones behind the glass. That will be harder to pull off without getting caught.

His aunt was practically hairless, even down there. He never saw another woman so sparsely haired, unless it was on purpose. He knows that sometimes women shave themselves. Lots of his movies have shown him that they do.

The last hooker he used was that way. That was why he'd ended up killing her. It wasn't planned; it was over before he realized what he was doing. I guess you could say it was an accident, but not the type you could own up to. The accident took place the winter before last. He hasn't used a woman since.

His mail girl knows the geranium woman. Boyo saw her coming out of the shop one afternoon last week. This makes sense to him. It connects.

Mail Girl Kyte has hanging plants in her yard too, but at least they're not geraniums.

# Chapter 12

"I love kissing." Beryl sighed luxuriously.

She stretched her arms above her head and opened her eyes just barely, to look at Dhani. She lay next to him on a blanket in St. Vital Park. On a grassy patch, almost dry.

"Kissing any old person?" Dhani asked.

"No," Beryl said. "Not any old person. Kissing you is pretty good, though." She realized, not for the first time, that if she was going to be spending time with Dhani, she would have to get better at thinking a bit before she spoke. He was very easy to get into trouble with. She wasn't sure she wanted to work that hard.

For instance now, Beryl didn't want to think just yet, didn't want to interrupt the light shimmering through her blood. She felt a little irritated with Dhani and his question at such a time, even though she had started it with her kissing comment.

He was the first man that Beryl had kissed since Georges. And that was two years ago and a bit. Georges had blown in from Montreal several years ago—transferred within the post office—and then blown away again three years later, to points further west. But not before capturing Beryl's heart.

Georges wanted to be free. Now and then Beryl had tried to talk to him about freedom being more a state of mind than a physical movement from say, Portage la Prairie, Manitoba to Lethbridge, Alberta. But Georges disagreed.

"I have to change my location from time to time," he said. "It's who I am."

Beryl wanted to laugh when he said stuff like that. After all, he was never wild and free enough to leave the post office behind. She got to thinking he was a phony towards the end. But he didn't know he was a phony, so she couldn't blame him.

On the day he was leaving she smiled to herself as she spread peanut butter on slices of whole wheat bread. Georges stood in her kitchen watching her.

"Are you making fun of me?" he asked, noticing her smile.

"No! God! No! I'm not making fun of you. I'm making sandwiches for you," Beryl had said.

"What are you thinking about?" Dhani asked now.

So Beryl told him about Georges.

"Do you miss him?" Dhani asked.

"No," she said. "Oh, I did at first. We'd been together almost three years. But Georges had these ideas about what made life good and none of them really agreed with mine."

"What do you think makes life good?" Dhani asked.

"Mmm. A comfortable couch. A fireplace. Chocolate."

Dhani pushed the hair back from Beryl's forehead and she hoped he wasn't thinking how ugly she looked in the light of the moon.

They lay near to where she had found the mushroom girl, but not too near. The night was warm after the hot day. The air wasn't going to cool down tonight.

"You look pretty," he said and Beryl thought he was lying.

"It was close to here that I found her," she said and sat up, shaking her fine blonde hair back over her forehead.

Dhani leapt up. He was brown and beautiful—an Indian, born in China, raised in England.

Beryl missed him terribly, even though he stood right there in front of her.

"We shouldn't be here!" Dhani struggled to whip the blanket out from under her.

"It wasn't that near," she said, scrambling to her feet.

Suddenly she felt that there was something missing from her, from the basic makeup of her personality. Or maybe not missing, but off somehow. Why didn't it bother her to be near the place, when it upset Dhani so much and he wasn't even the one who had found her? Maybe it did bother her and she was just too thick to know it. It would manifest itself physically in some way, like with a giant tumour growing inside her head. Something like that.

"We probably shouldn't even be in the same park," Dhani said, as he shook out the blanket. "The mosquitoes are terrible anyway!"

Beryl hurried after him with her sandals in her hand. I shouldn't have let myself go when we kissed, she thought. It was way too soon.

"Dhani, wait!" she cried. "I'm going to step on a wasp if I don't put my shoes on."

He slowed slightly. "Your shoes didn't protect you the last time."

Beryl felt as though it was her fault she had been stung by a wasp, her fault a girl was dead, and that Dhani judged her harshly for not having learned from either experience.

"What about all the other people in the park?" She gestured towards the shadowy figures of teenagers in the distance. "Should they not be here either?"

"It's not the same with them, Beryl. They're not connected to her like we are."

He stopped and touched her face when he said this, but he looked so sad when he did it that Beryl felt as though they might as well walk off in different directions.

"The only reason you're connected is because I told you about it," Beryl said and then wished she could erase the whine of her voice that hung between them in the night air.

They walked in silence the rest of the way to the car. Dhani started it up but didn't drive it anywhere.

"Beryl."

"Yes?"

"That's like saying, the only reason my mother and I are connected is that she gave birth to me."

"Yeah?"

"Beryl. Surely you see that connections go deeper than that."

"Well, yeah, of course. With the mother one anyway."

They were quiet for a few minutes as Dhani wheeled the car out onto River Road.

"If I think long enough about what you said, I know I'm going to start thinking that everything's connected to everything and that will drive me crazy," Beryl said. "It's all very well, but nothing really feels like that on a day-to-day basis.

"We shouldn't have kissed," she added.

Dhani looked at her and covered her hand with his. "Yes, we should have," he said. "Most definitely we should have."

Beryl sighed and leaned back in the seat. She found a lever and lifted it and the seat went all the way back.

"Let's go for a milkshake," Dhani said.

She closed her eyes and felt a warm breeze from the car windows fluttering across her bare legs. Dhani didn't believe in air conditioning and for the moment she was glad.

When she thought she heard him chuckle, she opened her eyes to check. He didn't look like he had, but the thought that he might have cheered her up and she began to think that perhaps their relationship wasn't irretrievably damaged.

"Beryl, sit up and fasten your seat belt, please."

She smiled and did as she was told.

"There's something wrong with me," she said and then wished very much she hadn't.

It was okay. Her words were lost in the mess Dhani made turning off Jubilee into the Bridge Drive-In. He cut across a lane of traffic without signalling and then made the turn in front of an oncoming car, again not using his signal and missing the other car by inches. Horns blasted, brakes screeched, and people screamed and gestured at him from their open windows.

"Goodness, Dhani!" Beryl said.

"I'm going to have chocolate tonight," he said as he wheeled into a parking spot, two spots really. He didn't drive very well at all. "What are you going to have?"

Beryl felt embarrassed as they walked toward the ice-cream stand. People were staring, wanting to get an up-close look at someone who drove so badly.

"I'll have peach," Beryl said. "Dhani, is it okay if I go and sit by the river and leave you to get the shakes?"

"Of course it is." He kissed her on the forehead. "I'll see you in a couple of minutes."

Beryl's knees shook a bit from Dhani's bad driving. She wondered if he had learned to drive in England and hadn't quite gotten the hang of driving on the right side of the road. She found an empty bench and sat down. Laughter floated across the water on the night air. Someone was having a party on a boat.

Beryl breathed deeply in the summer night, her gaze falling on the still waters of the Red River. The people on the boat, the party people, had the music turned up loud. It was Chris Isaak, singing about the world being on fire, singing about a wicked game that someone was playing.

Beryl ached inside at the sound of his voice. Deep inside, as deep as she went.

"I love this city," she whispered, as Dhani touched her bare arm with her cool peach milkshake. "There's no place on earth I'd rather be."

## Chapter 13

Hermione's shop, Cuts Only, was on Taché Avenue, across the street from the pool hall and down a ways. It was usually a dowdy little shop from the outside. But this summer the window boxes were bursting with geraniums, both at street level and upstairs where the owner lived. A riot of robust blooms spilled over the boxes and filled giant pots on either side of the door. Flower pots sat in the windows as well, both upstairs and down. Nothing but geraniums of many colours: crimson, coral, creamy white, lavender—grown, Beryl knew, for their varied scents as much as for their appearance.

Hermione was thin and bald and very definite about geraniums only and cuts only. No perms, no highlights, no colours, not even any blow drying. She had a dryer there so that if you wanted you could dry your own hair when it was cold outside, but it wasn't a service she offered.

"You want a blow job, honey, give it to yourself," Beryl had heard her bark more than once into the phone. She didn't have to be polite to everyone because she already had more customers than she could handle. She was a very fine hair cutter.

Hermione Rose had hauled Beryl in off the street one day and given her a haircut. That's how Beryl came to know her. Hermione'd had a cancellation; she couldn't abide cancellations.

She refused any payment; the haircut had been her idea. Beryl had thought she was months away from needing one.

Hermione regaled her with stories from her three marriages: one to a United Church minister—her first, so long ago she couldn't even conjure up his face; her second to an older man, already in his seventies when they tied the knot—he died on her; and the most recent marriage, this one to a woman named Lou. Hermione had thought this one was the real thing, till Lou ran off with the driver of the recycling truck.

Sometimes Hermione knew stuff was going to happen before it did, or so she said. Beryl didn't trust that kind of talk; she heard it all the time. People figuring they had some special thing happening, connecting them to a spirit world. Besides not trusting it, it made Beryl feel left out, jealous. Her own spiritual life was sadly lacking.

Hermione was a bit of a show-off, Beryl thought at first, but she didn't mind too much. It wasn't irritating like it was in some people.

Plus, it turned out to be the best haircut she ever had. She didn't need another one for a whole year, although Hermione disagreed with her on that point.

Sometimes Beryl would sit in Hermione's second chair and talk to her and her customer about her feeling that the world had gotten away on her. And most of the people in it. You could smoke there in the shop. Hermione encouraged it.

She had interesting magazines in her waiting area if you didn't feel like talking. There were *Life* magazines from the fifties, *Rolling Stone* from the seventies, Freak Brothers comics, and new stuff too: *Vanity Fair, Esquire, Mojo.* But there weren't any hair magazines for people to browse through and pick the cuts they liked. That was left to Hermione, who studied the face for a moment or two, asked a couple of what sometimes seemed to be irrelevant questions, and then started cutting.

Beryl had asked her once, after a customer left, what the colour of the woman's living-room drapes could possibly have to do with the cut she was going to get.

Hermione laughed.

"The colour of a person's drapes, whether they even own something called drapes, can tell you an enormous amount about that person. For instance, that woman looked at me as if I'd lost my marbles when I asked it—said she hadn't even heard the word since she visited her grandmother in Regina in 1971. It gives me an idea of who she is."

"I don't think you asked me any questions when I came in," Beryl said. "You just kind of ordered me around."

Hermione laughed again.

"Well, sometimes I just throw caution to the wind."

She busied herself with her next customer and Beryl thumbed through a *National Geographic* and smoked another cigarette.

What was it about her that made Hermione not ask her any questions that first day? She didn't want to be different from other people in the way she seemed. She wanted to talk about drapes or disparage drapes, the same as other customers. As it was, she didn't think she had any ideas about drapes at all and that worried her a little.

Hermione handed her customer, whose name was Jane, and who had a wrecked face, the old-fashioned hand mirror and twirled her about in the chair so she could view herself from all sides.

"Perfect," Jane said. "What do I owe you today, Herm?"

That was another thing about Hermione. She charged whatever she felt like. It often varied from day to day but it was never a lot, so no one complained.

"Ya know what, Jane?" she said. "I'm not gonna charge you today. I'm in an extra-good mood."

Jane laughed and her wrecked face looked worse. "You're serious, aren't you? Well, thank you, Herm, you're a wonder."

Beryl watched Jane stick a bill under the hand mirror when Herm's back was turned.

"What happened to her face?" Beryl asked when Jane was gone.

"I don't know," Hermione replied, pouring herself a cup of coffee. "Jane doesn't talk much. It's not really the type of question you come out and ask, is it?"

"No. I suppose not. It must be quite a life for her, being stared at all the time. I don't think I could take it," Beryl said.

"Yeah, you could," Hermione said and Beryl felt immediately better, for being thought of by this wondrous woman as someone who could manage life with a ruined face.

"Not me though, I couldn't do it," Hermione went on. "I'd shoot myself or slit my throat or whatever. Yup. Slit throat city."

When Beryl first met Hermione she worried that her new friend might have cancer and that was the reason she was bald. She hadn't asked her about it for the longest time, afraid to address disease, as so many people are. When she finally did ask, Hermione laughed.

"No. I don't have cancer yet, as far as I know. I just like the way I look with no hair. Besides, it was starting to go white and I'm not ready for that. I'll probably grow it again some day, but for now it suits me, it's easy, and it keeps the riff-raff away."

"What do you mean it keeps the riff-raff away?"

"I scare people with my look and I like it that way," Hermione had said. "There're so many weirdos out there."

Almost a week after what Beryl thought of as her kissing date with Dhani, the news broke as to the identity of the woman found murdered in the park. Her name was Beatrice Fontaine and she had lived in St. Boniface, near Happyland Pool.

The name didn't mean anything to Beryl—there was no reason it would—but it made the woman more real to her. Beatrice Fontaine had walked the same streets as Beryl, probably frequenting many of the same spots.

Beryl stopped in to see Hermione on her way home from work that day. She had started out by wanting to talk about Dhani, but that disappeared when she read about the mushroom girl in the *Free Press*.

Hermione knew, of course, that Beryl had found the body. But she didn't know about the mushrooms. The only people that Beryl had told so far were Stan and Dhani. It had been too big not to share with someone. She described the scene in the park now, as Hermione pushed her mop around beneath the chairs.

"Jesus," Hermione said. "Jesus fucking Christ. That's gotta be a horrifying picture to be carrying around inside your head. She formed a small pile of light brown hair and pushed it aside. "Bea was a customer of mine, you know," she went on.

"Really?" Beryl was stunned. She wouldn't be able to tell Dhani this particular piece of information. Talk about connections! He'd freak!

"Yeah. She was a sweet girl. Beautiful too. Imagine! God, I wish you hadn't told me about the mushrooms."

"Sorry. I…"

"No. No, it's okay. It's good you told me." Hermione propped her chin on the end of her mop. "I'll miss her. I hope they catch the guy and torture him."

"I wonder how she was killed," Beryl said, her voice shaky.

"I don't know. Here, sit down, honey, have some coffee." Hermione guided Beryl to a comfy chair in the waiting area and they sat awhile.

There were no customers and Hermione turned around her sign and locked the door.

"Herm?"

"Yeah?"

"Would you mind if I washed my hair?"

"Of course not. I'll even wash it for you. Come on."

"You don't have to help. Honest. I just kind of have this thing about washing my hair lately. It never feels really clean."

"Sit."

Hermione fastened a little black towel around Beryl's neck and ran very warm water through her hair till it was drenched. She squeezed shampoo into her hands and massaged it vigorously through Beryl's hair. It smelled like jasmine. She rinsed and rinsed and rinsed again.

The warm water felt good. Beryl wanted to talk about the mushrooms some more, but couldn't. She wanted to talk them to death, but the words wouldn't come.

Hermione wrapped a bigger towel around Beryl's head and kissed her on the cheek.

"There. Spanking clean," she said.

The distinct perfume of coconut lay underneath the tobacco smoke that clung to everything in the little shop. It was the geraniums. How did they thrive so in such an atmosphere? Beryl wondered. And then she looked at her friend and knew how. Hermione whispered to the plants and fussed about with a water spritzer and a fork, loosening soil, spraying the lush growth, caressing the foliage, sometimes crumbling a leaf in her fingers to release its scent.

This was the first summer she had put some of the plants outside. She had thought they would be too vulnerable out there, but Beryl had talked her into it. "They'll brighten the place up," she'd said.

"I kissed a guy I shouldn't have kissed," Beryl said, as she fluffed her hair about with the towel.

Hermione laughed. "What are you, in grade seven? I fucked ninety-two guys I shouldn'ta fucked. But there's nothing either of us can do about it. Let's have a real drink."

She retrieved a bottle of Jack Daniel's from a cupboard in her rolltop desk and poured them each a couple of inches.

Beryl said, "I'm going to ask you what you'll probably think is a stupid question."

"Shoot."

"Do you think it's significant that I found Beatrice Fontaine and that I also know you and that she was a customer of yours?"

"That's not a stupid question," Hermione said and took a long pull from her drink.

"Damn. I was afraid you'd say that."

"I don't know if it's significant in the grand scheme of things, but it's significant to me," Herm said.

"How?"

"I don't know yet."

"This guy I mentioned," Beryl said, "the one I kissed too soon? He's very big on connections between things being full of all kinds of meaning."

"He sounds interesting," Herm said. "Maybe I could fuck him next."

Beryl smiled. "Yeah, he is interesting in an irritating sort of way. I quite like him."

"Maybe it's okay that you kissed him already," Hermione said gently.

"I don't know…a passionate kiss sort of knocks down a barrier, doesn't it? Maybe that barrier shouldn't have been knocked down yet. Or ever, even. It changes everything. I can't believe it isn't the same for him. He seems so…sensitive, with all his talk of connections."

"I think you might be exaggerating the importance of kissing," said Hermione.

"No. I'm not."

"Well, maybe his whole world has changed too."

"Are you making fun of me?"

"No."

"A kiss shouldn't take place only because it seems the thing to do at the time," Beryl said. "It's more important than that."

She came away from the shop feeling a little bit better and a little bit drunk. On the walk home she tried to organize her thoughts and couldn't. Who cares? she thought, as she passed through Coronation Park. Who cares how organized I am if I feel better and my hair's clean? Besides, Dhani sucked wasp poison out of my foot; it's okay that I let myself go when we kissed.

## Chapter 14

Dhani spoke like a Canadian; he'd been here that long. This was a disappointment for Beryl. She wanted an accent to go along with his exotic beauty.

On her deck with Dhani she could forget the mushroom girl and a lot of other things besides. She could almost imagine she was someone else, living in a foreign land sipping strong coffee.

It was a quiet morning a week after their night in the park. The occasional car washed by on the drive and the crows shouted in one of their many voices. But that was streets away. It was peaceful here. Beryl was reminded of mornings when she was a kid. When she'd had chicken pox, or mumps, or some other childhood disease. It had been good to miss school, but eerily lonesome on her own outside the school walls.

"So, the girl you found in the park?"

Dhani didn't look at Beryl when he spoke. He talked to the grand old willow tree that shaded most of the deck.

"Beatrice Fontaine, you mean."

He looked at her now but didn't speak.

"Dhani, what is it? You look horrible. Please tell me this isn't about the terrible mistake I made in letting us lie down too close to where I found her."

He couldn't possibly know about the Hermione connection, could he?

"No, Beryl," he said. "No. I'm afraid we're connected to her in more ways than one or two."

"What do you mean, Dhani? What are you talking about?"

"I know someone who actually knew the girl."

"You do?"

"Yes."

They called her a girl but she was really a woman. Thirty-three years old on the day she died on the spot where Beryl found her.

"You must have just found out," Beryl said. "It was only in the paper yesterday, who she was and all."

"Yes."

"Who is it that knew her? Someone close to you?"

"Well, not really. I don't actually know her. Shirley at work does. She went through pharmacy with this woman that knew the dead girl."

Beryl breathed an inward sigh of relief. This had nothing to do with her or Hermione. It struck her as very unreasonable that she had to hide the Hermione connection from Dhani but she knew she did, for her own sake. Dhani was definitely very odd in this particular area.

"Wait," she said. "Shirley at work went through pharmacy with a woman who knew Beatrice."

"Yes. This friend of hers, acquaintance really, remembers filling a prescription for her a year or two ago. She thought she recognized the name and looked it up in their computer and bingo."

"Bingo?"

"Yes," Dhani said. "Just as she suspected, the girl had been a customer at the pharmacy where she works."

"What's this person, this pharmacist's name?" Beryl asked. She reached in her pocket for a cigarette.

"I don't know," Dhani said, "but I could find out."

"No," Beryl said. "It's not necessary. Dhani, don't you see how tenuous a connection this is? It doesn't matter. Surely to God it doesn't matter."

She lit her cigarette with a wooden match and inhaled deeply. It was the first time she had lit up in Dhani's presence, although she had warned him that she was likely to do so from time to time.

"Of course it matters," Dhani said, talking to the willow tree again. "I wish you wouldn't smoke, Beryl."

"I wish you weren't insane," Beryl muttered.

"Pardon?"

"Nothing."

They were quiet for a while with the wind in the trees.

"Hi, Beryl!"

It was the little boy from two doors down on the north side, calling in from the front sidewalk.

"Hi, Russell! How're things?"

Beryl was glad to see him. Maybe he would come over and blow some of his spit bubbles for them and Dhani would see that there were better things to occupy his mind than his non-existent connections.

"Who's that man?" Russell asked.

"This is my friend, Dhani," Beryl said. "Would you like to come and meet him?"

Dhani tried to smile but it wasn't good enough for young Russ.

"No, thanks," he said and pedalled his trike on up the street.

"Bye, Beryl!" he hollered over his shoulder.

"So long, Russell!"

"Your glumness has scared away my neighbour," Beryl said.

"Sorry."

Beryl concentrated on blowing her smoke in the opposite direction of Dhani. He took a good deal of the fun out of having a cigarette.

"Even if all these feeble connections do mean something," she said, "and it's obvious they do mean something to you, what are we, or you, supposed to do about it?"

Dhani sighed and sipped his coffee.

"You like your coffee very strong," he said.

"Yes. You don't, I guess."

"No."

"Is it a religious thing, this thing about connections? Is it part of a religion I could read about or you could explain to me?"

"No, Beryl, it's just me. It's just a thing I have."

For such a smart guy Dhani could be a real bonehead at times. She almost said it out loud but stopped herself in time. She figured one sentence like that could be enough for someone as sensitive as Dhani. And she wasn't sure she wanted to lose him, not yet anyway.

"You have a picture of her," he said. "At least, I assume it's her."

Beryl's scalp tingled.

"How do you know that, Dhani?"

She was suddenly not so sure she couldn't stand to lose this person who had obviously been rifling through her desk drawers.

"Where did you get it, Beryl?"

"How do you know about it, Dhani?"

"I'm worried about you, Beryl."

"I think you should go now, Dhani."

He didn't move.

"Hi, Beryl!"

It was Russell again, this time on foot. He had come up silently, through the yard.

"Russell, you scared the living daylights out of me," Beryl said.

The little boy leaned with his elbows on the deck and blew a big beautiful bubble made of spit.

Beryl and Dhani both laughed and Russell laughed too.

"My mum told me not to blow bubbles anymore," he said and blew another one bigger than the last.

"Well, you should probably listen to what your mother says." Dhani crouched down near the boy and stuck out his hand. "I'm Dhani," he said, "a friend of Beryl's."

Russell smiled shyly and gave him his sticky little hand.

"Hello, Dhani," he said and skipped away down the sunny street.

Beryl stood up. It was definitely time for Dhani to leave. She needed to think. She needed to ponder alone for awhile: was Dhani crazy? Was she falling for a crazy person?

She waved half-heartedly from her kitchen window as she watched his silver Camry back into the Kruck-Boulbrias' garbage cans. He knocked them right over. At least he had the decency to get out and place them back in position, even if he blocked the lane while doing so, causing a short line-up of people in their cars to wait patiently while he completed his task. No one honked, no one shouted—Beryl was pleased with her neighbours.

## Chapter 15

Beryl's ankles hurt on the walk home from the bus stop. Her plan was to rest for a bit with her feet up on cushions, have a bite to eat—maybe a bowl of Corn Pops—and then spend an hour or so deadheading her lobelia. It was one of her favourite activities. The weather had been hot and dry for a few days and the flowers were begging to be done. She had promised them and the bees as she left the house this morning.

When Beryl entered the yard an uneasy feeling caught in her throat, slowed her in her tracks. Nothing happened, no one spoke; there was no noise at all. Just a feeling. I've been hanging around with Dhani too much, she thought. All his talk of vibes and karma, those sorts of things; it's rubbing off.

She found her key underneath the flower pot and looked over her shoulder as she unlocked the door.

"This is stupid," she said out loud. I may as well leave the doors open if I'm going to leave the key in such an obvious place.

She resolved to give that some thought.

Once her feet were out of their socks and shoes her ankles felt better. Beryl threw on a pair of overalls and decided to forgo putting her feet up and eating some Corn Pops. I'll get right at the lobelia, she planned, as she tossed her postal uniform down the basement stairs. That'll fix me up.

She poured herself a Dr. Pepper over ice and headed back outside.

The hanging plant closest to the door seemed the safest place to start. Close, and she could work her way out. The flowers were so abundant and beautiful they dazzled Beryl for a moment. She couldn't see them as individuals, hundreds of them needing their tired dead blooms removed to make room for the new. As she focussed her eyes and blinked, and blinked again, she couldn't find a single bloom that was past its best. This was impossible. She hadn't tended her flowers in several days.

The yard was too quiet. Beryl couldn't even hear traffic noise from across the river. No trains ran and no birds sang.

She feared she was losing her mind. She moved on to the next planter, this one lobelia mixed with petunias, and stared into the blue blooms. Not a one needed doing. Not a one was less than perfect.

Slowly, she walked around her yard knowing what she was going to find. Someone had been here and someone had deadheaded her lobelia, all of them. There wasn't a dead flower to be found.

It must have taken whoever did it well over an hour unless he or she had help. A sidekick deadheader. Maybe one of the neighbours had seen something. That was her only hope.

She wanted to think it was a friend who had done her a favour but she knew it wasn't. Anyone who was her friend knew how she felt about this chore. She loved it! Someone had either intentionally ruined her fun or, worse, was terrorizing her in a way so subtle it made the hair on her arms stand up.

Beryl walked around to the front of her house and sat down on the deck in the shade of the Russian willow. This was an impossible situation. She couldn't phone the police: "Yes, I'd like to report some lobelia that have been deadheaded."

To wait a bit seemed a good idea, to let the situation settle. Maybe she herself had done it and forgotten. No. Maybe it hadn't happened and her eyes were playing tricks on her. She got up and looked again at each planter in the yard, abundant with the healthy blue flowers. No.

She doubted she could even tell a friend. It was too weird. If she tried to explain it to anyone they would think she was nuts. Tending flowers wasn't what criminals did.

Dhani! She could tell Dhani! She felt a sudden rush of love for her new friend, the one who caused her so much trouble and worry. It filled her up quite unexpectedly. He was just odd enough and in exactly the right way, to understand the importance of this situation.

She phoned him at the pharmacy. He had booked off for the morning and still hadn't made it in. They had just heard from him; he was on his way. The lovely feelings she had, ever so briefly, evaporated. Dhani was the culprit. Who else? She even remembered telling him about her love of deadheading. It struck her that it was precisely the type of thing he would do. But why? As punishment for not agreeing with him about everything? Had she disparaged him?

Maybe he wasn't her friend anymore. Definitely a possibility since the other day and their argument about… What had they argued about? The part that stayed with her was him opening a drawer in her kitchen desk to have a look inside. She wished so much that he hadn't done that.

She tried to look at it in a different light: if she was alone in Dhani's kitchen would she open a drawer in his desk? Yes, she would. But only if he was nowhere in the vicinity, only if there was no chance in this lifetime that he would find out. So all that meant was that she was a more devious person than Dhani. At least he was honest about nosing around in her private stuff.

But he had confronted her with what he'd found! Surely that was wrong. It was one thing to come clean about his despicable behaviour but quite another to gloss over it and start accusing Beryl. If he was going to admit to rifling through her drawers he could at least do so with cap in hand.

Beryl realized she didn't even know where Dhani lived. It was hard to picture his kitchen, his kitchen drawers and what he kept inside of them. She expected they'd be tidy. But really, she didn't know very much about him at all.

He was behind the prescription counter at the drugstore when she finally tracked him down later in the afternoon. She wanted to see if he could account for his whereabouts in the morning. And he could, unless he was lying. But she didn't think he was; it wasn't his style. She was both relieved and disappointed. In a way, she wanted it to be Dhani who had tended her flowers. It wouldn't feel so dangerous if it was him.

"I was at the toe doctor," he said.

"The toe doctor? You don't have any toes."

Dhani didn't respond and Beryl felt terrible. "Sorry," she said.

"Once a year or so I check in with the orthopedic surgeon who removed my toes."

"So, how is everything?"

"Okay." He shrugged. "With my toes, anyway."

There were no customers, but Dhani busied himself with something. The counter was so high that Beryl couldn't tell what he was up to. She wondered why pharmacy counters were so tall.

She turned away, changing her mind about confiding in him.

"Beryl, wait. What did you want to ask me?"

"Nothing," she said. "Never mind."

"What do you mean nothing? You phoned me here. Now you come and interrupt my work for no good reason? What the frick, Beryl?"

"'Frick' isn't a word," she said sadly. "Why can't you just say fuck, like other people?"

"Why are you being so nasty?" Dhani asked.

"You're the nasty one," Beryl said, and her eyes filled with tears. She turned to leave.

"Beryl, don't go!"

"You know what, Dhani?" she said over her shoulder, "Frick off."

She didn't shout it, she just said it, and not very loudly. Probably Dhani was the only one to hear.

"Beryl." He looked crestfallen.

Why couldn't she manage to stay mad at this man for more than a few minutes at a time, she wondered. She came back. "I don't even know where you live," she said.

"On Palmerston."

"Palmerston is one of my favourite streets."

"Is it?"

"Yeah. Do you live on the river side?"

"Yes, I do."

"Oh, Dhani."

"What are you doing this coming weekend?" he asked. "Do you want to do something with me?"

"Oh. I'm going to the folk festival."

She considered inviting him to go with her and Stan and the others. But she didn't really want to. If he came with them she'd end up worrying about him, feeling responsible for him. And for sure they'd fight some more. She just wanted to go and enjoy herself for awhile and hopefully not worry about anything at all—forget about a few things if possible. Maybe not Dhani, but certain aspects of him for sure.

"I'll see you when I get back?" she said.

"I hope so."

## Chapter 16

When night begins to fall, Boyo removes the wiry grey wig from his head and places it on the dummy. In the dusky light of the bedroom he lifts the cotton dress over his head and places it, too, on the tall slender mannequin he took from a dumpster out behind the old Eaton's store downtown. It isn't stealing if it's already garbage.

The dress is due for a wash, he realizes as he straightens the collar; he can smell himself on it. It is an unpleasant smell that he knows comes from the bad part inside him, the geranium part. He unbuttons the flowery dress and throws it across his bedroom into the hall.

There are no lights on upstairs; he moves about in the growing darkness. Turning back to the female figure, he runs his hands over the hips and the smooth part between the legs, nothing messy there to ruin it.

Suddenly a street lamp flickers on outside and shines its light on the face of Auntie Hort. He runs his fingers over his own art work on the front of the head. It had needed more of a face than the boring bumps and slopes that the mannequin manufacturers had come up with. It needed Auntie Cunt's face.

He touches the eyebrows that are raised in a permanent look of surprise. And the wide-open black eyes that go along with them. Why the surprise all the time? What was so startling about the boring little life that they lived together? Was she surprised to see him rise from his bed on one more morning? Shocked that he made it home from school in one piece? Was it so amazing that he ate the food on his plate, cleaned up the dishes afterward and headed out to the garage, night after night after tedious night?

And what was so puzzling and wrong about a young boy wanting…no, needing, a glass of water? It was just one more way that she could deny him

No one on the planet could have been gladder of anything than he was of his Aunt Hortense's death. He was just eighteen when it happened and he didn't comprehend that her death, welcome as it was, cut his moorings out from under him. He was totally alone.

Any feeble attempts that he had made at friendship over the years had turned out badly.

Hort had discouraged friends, both male and female. She had none of her own and wouldn't hear of Boyo bringing anyone home. "We don't want people knowing our business," she said.

There was Kenny Mathes two doors down. Kenny and he had managed some games of soldiers and catch for part of one summer, but Boyo stole one of Kenny's Dinky toys and then lied, pretending the tiny dump truck was his own. Kenny grew tired of Boyo's lies. When he heard him telling a new kid on the block that his own name was Kenny Mathes it freaked out the real Kenny so badly that he didn't want to play with Boyo anymore.

And Mrs. Snider, across the back lane, caught Boyo snipping the whiskers off their cat, Peppie. She forbade her boys to play with him after that and spread it around the neighbourhood that he was bad.

Boyo had been looking for hair to glue on his doll, to glue on its private parts. The cat's whiskers seemed a good idea. But after Mrs. Snider yelled at him and told his aunt on him, he settled for pulling his own eyebrows out and using them. What did you need eyebrows for, anyway?

It was after that that Hort threatened to give him away. She frightened him with words that conjured up the blackest, deepest hole he could imagine. The hole folded in on itself, over and over, till it was a size that he could swallow. So he did swallow and he held it down, along with his shame, his guilt, and his fear; along with burning rage and hot desire and all the tears he wasn't allowed to shed. It lived dark and hard inside the slimy home provided by his tender gut.

Her death happened on its own, without his help. Her heart had been weak, he was told, after the autopsy. Still, she was young to suffer a heart attack, they said, just forty-eight. They were sorry; he wasn't.

Even after all these years he is still glad. He's thirty-four years old now and his gladness hasn't wavered.

Hortense even looked surprised in death, he recalls now, until he managed to shut the eyes. Her head rested, face up on the wide flat rim of the bathtub.

He remembers what that felt like, touching her eyes.

The eyeballs themselves first, just to see what they felt like. It might be his only chance to do such a thing, or so he thought at the time. And then he touched the paper thin lids, cool by then. They wouldn't stay closed.

He went out to the back alley and got two stones to weigh them down, to keep them from flipping open.

And then he phoned the funeral parlour. He figured since she was already dead there was no point wasting money on an ambulance. But the funeral parlour people didn't see it that way. They told him he had to phone somebody other than them—like 911—they even offered to do it for him, figuring he was upset, he supposed. He asked them then if he could drive the old lady over himself but they seemed aghast at that suggestion and assured him they wouldn't receive her if he did.

He was tempted just to bury the old crow out in the yard with the bones of her stupid budgie birds. But he knew he'd be suspected of foul play if he did that. God, why did it have to be so complicated? Where was a good solid ice floe when you needed one?

The water in the bathtub was yellowish with her piss. Bits of cloudy shit muddied it further. He let the water out, putting on a rubber glove to do so, not wanting to touch the Hort soup that she had made.

He decided not to cover her up before the paramedics came; he wanted her exposed. With his rubber-gloved hand he adjusted one bony knee, spread her skinny legs ever so slightly to give her a disgustingly wanton air.

When everyone had left, he opened Birdie's cage. She was the latest in a long line of budgies who had all been named Birdie. Boyo reached in and wrapped his hand around the green-hued bird. He took it outside to the back stoop along with Hort's old meat cleaver. And under the bright July sun, with one swift motion, he took Birdie's head off. Then he turned on the hose and cleaned up the mess he had made, flushing both parts of the budgie into the flower bed. It felt good, like a celebration.

Boyo fumbles in his closet now for a clean outfit for his mannequin. As he buttons up the dress a peppery geranium scent fills his nostrils, fills his whole head. He shivers.

When the mannequin is properly attired Boyo retrieves the soiled dress from the hall floor and places it in the clothes hamper in the bathroom. Then he goes downstairs and stretches out on the old maroon couch in the living room. He tries to fall asleep; it's what he needs. Maybe in sleep he can get away from the blood-red geraniums and the tall women. This thing may be the end of me, he thinks, as he drifts off. Perhaps that isn't so bad.

## Chapter 17

It was the final night of the Winnipeg Folk Festival in Birds Hill Park, northeast of the hot prairie city. Beryl sat in the last rays of the setting sun on a striped blue chair, the kind that lies right on the ground so you don't sit too tall. It was thirty-two in the shade and even in her coolest dress, the one Dhani had complimented her on, she could feel the sweat drip down her sides.

She missed him, even though she hadn't invited him to come along. She longed to see him again, to kiss him again. His lips were so soft. When she had phoned to say she was sorry for her behaviour at the drugstore, he apologized first and they ended up laughing. And when she told him about her lobelia, it worried him. He said it was something that shouldn't be taken lightly. Then he suggested calling the police and she said she didn't want to and they had ended up fighting again.

Her feelings for Dhani were so strong. She could remember hints of feeling this way before, but not with all the extras, both good and bad. It seemed complicated to her, but she recognized that that was partly due to the murder. It had a way of moving in and muddying up any clarity of vision she could get going.

Beryl wiped her forehead with the back of her hand and stood up with a sigh.

"I'm going to see about doing some drinking and smoking," she said to the four people she had come with: Stan Socz, his wife

Raylene, Stan and Raylene's new neighbour, Yolanda Cramer, and a man named Wally Goately. A distant relative of Stan's wife, Wally had recently insinuated himself into their lives.

Beryl had met Raylene before, at post office Christmas parties, but she didn't know her well. And this was her first meeting with Yolanda. She was in a wheelchair and Beryl wondered if that was why Stan had invited her. It got you a good spot near the stage.

"I'll come with you." Wally leapt up and so did Stan.

Raylene glared at her husband. She obviously felt someone should stay with Yolanda.

Yolanda caught it. "You go too, Raylene. I'm perfectly happy where I am."

"No. I think I'll stay put for now. I want to see Oscar Lopez and I think he's next."

Raylene was a good person. And less twitchy than the three scruffy travellers heading west to the drinks tent. She and Stan had hired a babysitter for the night, for their young daughter, Ellie. Beryl hoped Raylene didn't resent her going off with Stan or Stan going off with her or anything at all.

The first drink went down fast and Beryl ordered another. Once it was in her hands she leaned back against the picnic table and felt the rough wood under her thighs and the comfort of her good friend, Stan, beside her. She knew very little about Wally except his ridiculous last name, but if he belonged to Stan and Raylene, he was all right with her.

The tequila spread its magic to every dark corner of her body. It unclenched her heart and knocked down the barbed wire around her eyes, flattened it. It blew through her brain like a warm dry westerly, soaking up her mucky fears, clearing the way for light and space. She'd pay heavily for this, but Jesus Christ Almighty, it was worth it!

She asked Wally about his last name.

"Goately?" she asked.

"Yeah, I'm afraid so."

"I've never heard that name before."

"And you're not likely to again. At one time it was Golately. At least that's what my aunt told me. A spelling error at immigration stuck, way back in 1848 or so. And the idiot ancestor let it go, didn't bother to change it. And a succession of idiots ever since, including me, have also let it go."

"Isn't this great?" Stan said. He stretched his long legs out in front of him and stared at the women walking by. "Look at all the breasts. God, I love the folk festival."

"I think my aunt was lying," Wally went on. "And that our name was always Goately. As in goat. Because I come from goat herders or more likely people who behaved like goats or maybe even were goats themselves. My great-great-great-great grandfather was a goat."

Beryl laughed out loud.

"What if Yolanda has to take a crap while she's here?" Wally said out of the blue. "With her wheelchair and all." He looked anxiously from Stan to Beryl; he was deadly serious.

Beryl stared at Wally with interest.

"Good question," Stan said. "I checked that out with her before we came. She won't have to, apparently. How exactly she knows this, I don't know, but it's not something we're going to have to think about."

"How can she know for sure?" Wally asked. "It's a long haul till the end of the evening concert."

"What did you say when you checked it out with her, Stan?" Beryl asked. "How did you word it?"

"I just said that the washroom facilities probably wouldn't be all that easy for her to maneuvre and how did she feel about that and she said not to worry, that she wouldn't have to make use of them. That was good enough for me."

"She's munching on Raylene's fresh peas," Wally said, "and on your cherries, Beryl. I wouldn't be too surprised if they had some sort of effect."

"Don't worry, Wally." Beryl patted his bony shoulder. "Even if she does have to have a dump later on, it's nothing you're going to have to be involved in directly."

Wally didn't look so sure. "What if it comes upon her when all you guys are off doing something and I'm the only one around?" he said. "What then?"

"Let's smoke some dope." Beryl stood up and stretched.

"Good idea!" Wally and Stan said in unison.

They bought more drinks and transferred them to their travelling mugs before heading out to a grassy area beyond some trees. There were fewer people around but there was a lot of space to keep them company.

The sun was barely down and the sky was fantastic in the west, too beautiful to be real. Beryl hoped it wasn't the result of deadly toxins in the atmosphere. Summer sunsets had taken a turn for the other-worldly: this one was a shining kingdom in the sky. Or so it seemed to Beryl.

"Look at that sky," she whispered.

She filled her pipe and fired it up, holding the hit deep in her lungs. She watched the hash burn as she handed the pipe to Stan. They sucked on it, the three of them, till they heard Jann Arden's voice sailing over the countryside. Then they headed back and Beryl plopped herself down in a spot away from the congestion of the main stage crowd. It felt better back here.

"See!" Wally stared down at her with his hands on his hips. "See what I mean! It'll be very easy for us to find ourselves in different places. I just know I'm gonna have to take her to the crapper."

Beryl stood up. "Sorry, Wally. I wasn't thinking."

Stan shook his head. "Beryl should be allowed to sit back here if she wants to."

"No, she shouldn't," Wally said, as they stepped their way back through the sea of tarps and blankets. "Not in these special circumstances."

"Jesus, Wally," Stan said. "The circumstances hardly qualify as special."

"Yeah, they do."

Beryl chuckled. She felt okay about being needed even if it was by a shamefully neurotic distant relative of a friend's wife.

Besides, it sometimes cheered her up to be in the company of someone more fucked up than herself.

Yolanda and Raylene were chatting and swatting their way through Jann Arden's performance.

"I thought the skeeters were supposed to die when it gets this hot." Raylene slathered herself with insect repellent.

"That's just a prairie myth," Yolanda said, "like it doesn't snow when it gets really cold."

Beryl looked at Yolanda's ankles. They looked to be covered with ants. But it was getting dark and she couldn't be sure that she wasn't imagining it. It could be drug-related, she supposed.

"Do you want me to spray some of this stuff on your ankles Yolanda? It looks like you're being eaten alive...I think."

Yolanda laughed. "Thanks, Beryl, but no. I can't feel my ankles so it doesn't really matter. One of the benefits of being paralyzed in certain areas." She laughed again and Beryl smiled.

Jann Arden was talking about bowel movements. Beryl saw Wally looking at Yolanda out of the corner of his eye. He sat as far away from them as he could on a corner of the tarpaulin, long arms clutching his pointy knees, a tall man folded in three. Beryl sat down beside him and put her arm around him. God, he was skinny!

"Are you okay, Wally?"

"No, not really." A painful smile flickered for a second. "I don't think I like the folk festival. It's too rustic for me.

"And I'm too close to other people." He shrugged and Beryl let go of him, backed off a little.

Wally glanced over both shoulders. "I don't like being too close. I keep thinking I'm gonna step on a baby or something."

"Maybe you could lie back and try getting into the music," Beryl suggested. "Forget about all these people for a while."

She made a pillow for him from her backpack and Wally lay stiffly back against it.

"Thank you, Beryl," he said quietly. "I'm sorry."

# Chapter 18

It was very dark as Beryl carefully made her way back to their camp near the stage. She had gone for popcorn, lots of it, and she left a little trail behind her as she walked.

For a few minutes she couldn't find the spot because no one was there. Not even Yolanda in her wheelchair.

Then she saw Wally, hugging his knees, staring not at the stage, but at something in his own head that Beryl was glad she didn't have to see.

She sat. Los Lobos were playing "Down by the River." She munched on the popcorn and offered some to Wally, who shook his head. The popcorn was stale. Beryl considered returning it to the popcorn man for a refund.

"Where is everyone?" she asked. "Where's Yolanda?"

"They've taken her to the loo," Wally said.

Everything suddenly seemed a bit weird to Beryl and she couldn't settle in to the music.

"Down by the river, I shot my baby," Los Lobos sang.

"They've taken Yolanda to the loo," Wally repeated, louder this time.

"Yeah. Thanks, Wally. I heard you the first time!" Beryl stood up and someone behind her heaved a sigh.

"Sorry," she said, gathering up her popcorn. She had decided to return it; she had spent seven dollars. If the popcorn man made a fuss, she would write a letter to the editor.

As Beryl moved through the crowd she kept an eye out for her friends. She wished Stan would appear.

She stood at the edge of the food area, rethinking her decision about the popcorn. It made her uncomfortable. Maybe if she was pleasant, yet firm, the popcorn man wouldn't give her too much trouble.

There was a lineup.

Joe Paine was in it, standing alone, looking rigid and stern. Beryl was pretty sure he hadn't seen her. She turned around and, tossing her popcorn into a garbage bin, walked quickly off in the opposite direction. She had trouble relating the sight of Joe to the veterinarian that everyone raved about. He was so tall, taller even than Wally, who must have been over six feet when he wasn't slouching. He had a terrible slouch. There seemed to be a lot of tall thinness going around.

"Dead. Ooh, I shot her dead." Los Lobos sang on. A Neil Young song. Beryl wondered if the guys in the band knew they were in Neil's home town.

She decided to use the washroom before heading back. It was pitch black inside and not the sort of place you wanted to feel your way around in. She hoped Yolanda had made out all right.

By the time Beryl got back to their spot, Stan, Raylene, and Yolanda were comfortably ensconced, listening to something soft and beautiful coming from the stage. Beryl was so glad to see them she felt a little wobbly in the knees. She sat close to Stan, hoping Raylene wouldn't think it was too close. Wally was gone.

"Joe Paine is here," she said, but not loudly enough for anyone to hear.

# Chapter 19

Fear shook Beryl awake in the night. It loomed huge behind her eyes. Fear coursed through her veins; it was in her blood.

While she slept someone had stitched a soggy balloon, heavy with toxic waste, behind her eyes; that's how it felt. It dripped down her throat and spread poison through her system.

When morning finally came, she phoned in to book off work.

"Is it your feet?" Ed, her supervisor, asked.

"Pardon?"

"Is it your feet again? Have you maybe stepped on a rusty nail this time?"

"No. No, nothing like that," she said. "This is more of an inside-of-me sickness."

"Will you be seeing a doctor?" Ed asked.

"What? I don't know. No, I doubt very much if it'll come to that."

After putting down the phone Beryl sat and stared at the toaster for awhile. She didn't want to be famous for her feet.

She stepped out the back door to look at the day, checking first to make sure no one was about. Her body quivered with unease as she reached for the newspaper, lips pressed together to protect the teeth that she pictured being whacked out of her head with a baseball bat. She wouldn't have the energy for false teeth; she'd rather die.

It was a clear, sharp-edged morning. Clouds would have been better. Drizzle even, but not rain. She would have to think about rain and she didn't want to think on this day, not about anything. Thinking was what hurt.

Sticking the newspaper under her arm, she held her wrists with opposite hands as best she could, to prevent her hands being lopped off by a stray axe or power saw. She wouldn't have the energy for prosthetic devices. She'd rather be dead.

This was Beryl having a hangover. This was how she paid.

A bird fell out of the sky and landed at her feet. A crow. It was huge and it was dead. She'd seen plenty of dead birds in her time; they were always banging into glass in the city. But this one hadn't banged into anything. It seemed to die of natural causes at Beryl's feet.

This must happen all the time, she thought, birds plummeting from the sky—landing next to unsuspecting people. I'm surprised it hasn't happened to me before. At least it didn't land on my head.

It felt more significant than that, but Beryl wouldn't think about it now, not till after a couple more sleeps, when her hangover had faded and her thoughts were better connected to the real world.

She couldn't touch the bird, so she left it there on her doorstep. Hopefully it would disappear during the course of the day while she hid behind closed doors. And if it didn't, she would figure out what to do about it later. Maybe she could carry it in a shovel to the river.

What if the crow moved? What if it wasn't dead? What if she was so afraid of death that she couldn't help a dying creature in its last moments? No. It was a goner. In all her life she had only seen one other thing look more dead than this crow. A picture of the mushroom girl tangled itself up in the swamp inside her brain.

There's alive and there's dead. And there's the moment when life leaves the body. It was that moment that Beryl feared today and she didn't know why. It had something to do with power that wasn't hers; it had something to do with everything.

She rubbed her eyes, hard. These were the kinds of thoughts she wanted to put on hold till she felt better. These and thoughts that the bird was especially for her.

The folk festival wasn't something she wanted to think about either. Or Wally; he seemed so lame to her. A wave of nausea welled up inside Beryl when she thought about him, but maybe it wasn't related. She must remember not to mention her thoughts about Wally to Stan. He was always accusing her of not liking anyone.

Joe Paine was at the folk festival. That was something else she didn't want to think about.

The phone rang and Beryl jumped. What if it was Joe? What if he had changed his mind about not wanting to bother her anymore? She let the answering machine take it.

It was Dhani, wanting to talk about their "differences," as he put it.

They hadn't seen each other since the day in the drugstore, the day of the lobelia.

Beryl watched the machine as Dhani talked, but she didn't feel up to picking up the phone. It might make her feel worse and she didn't think she could go on living if she felt any worse. She needed to talk to someone, but not Dhani. Maybe Hermione, but later.

"Come on, Beryl," Dhani said. "I bet you're standing right there looking at the machine. I know you're at home because I called you at work and they said you were sick. Pick up, please. I won't ask anything of you or accuse you of anything. I shouldn't have criticized you for lying to the police and I'm sorry. Anyway, give me a call."

What the hell was he talking about?

He recited his phone number twice and Beryl didn't write it down either time. She had it, anyway; he should know that by now.

She sat down at the kitchen table and forced herself to think hard enough to figure out what Dhani was talking about. They'd had so many fights since he'd accused her of lying to the police that she could hardly fathom that being the thing he picked to apologize for. Maybe he was totally cuckoo in a polite, quiet sort of way.

A hot shower made Beryl feel better for the few minutes that it lasted. She arranged a towel on her pillow and crawled back into bed. Even there, some days, she feared for her dependable teeth and fragile wrists. There was nothing special about either her hands or her teeth. It was just that for some reason, maybe some long-ago dream that stuck with her, she feared for their loss.

She drifted off with a Robert Frost poem front and centre in her brain. The one called "Out, Out," where a boy loses his hand to a power saw and the life rushes out of him.

Beryl dreamed about her mother.

*When she enters the dark apartment, she sees the familiar soft white hair. A feeling of tenderness rushes through her and she is relieved to see the television set tuned to Canada AM. A good sign that her mum is still interested in something. And her hair looks so clean. Maybe I'll hug her, Beryl thinks, kiss her. Maybe we'll have a conversation.*

*She pushes further into the room, through the thick dank air full of her mother's filth. When she comes even with the chair, the one with the up and down switch that makes life so grand, her mother turns her head so that Beryl can see her face.*

*It's worse than any live face she has ever seen. The skin is the texture of a cantaloupe, the outer rind. And the eyes are yellow. Yellow eyes that don't see at first and then do, and it was better when they were blind. Her head bobs. Bobs a lot. A bobbing head like a diseased marionette. An evil puppet.*

*"Fine, thanks," growls the monster head in a deep voice Beryl has never heard before. Fine, thanks.*

She awoke and stumbled from her bed. The dead bird was better than this.

# Chapter 20

Beryl walked home from work on Thursday and as she crossed the two rivers she began making plans for a party. She wanted to have it when it was still summer so her guests could be outside on the deck. Stan should meet Dhani. Hermione should meet Dhani. They would probably have a lot in common.

Then Beryl remembered the secret she was keeping from Dhani, about Beatrice Fontaine being Herm's customer, and she realized she couldn't chance a meeting between the two of them. Dhani would accuse Beryl of all kinds of things. Maybe she should tell him. Or was it too late?

Who was she kidding? There could be no party. Not till the killer was found, anyway, and maybe not even then. Unless she left Dhani off the invitation list, which seemed kind of stupid since he was her favourite person in the world right now.

Beryl decided not to have a party. Somebody else could have a party.

As she entered her street she kept an eye out for her cat, Jude, who had slipped out on her this morning when she hadn't had time to catch her. There was a by-law in Winnipeg outlawing cats on the streets, so Beryl was a little worried about Jude, a white Siamese with beige tips. She hoped Jude hadn't been trapped by a vengeful neighbour.

Then she saw her cat, bright in the summer sunshine, sitting in the middle of the sidewalk several houses away. Jude bounded towards her and rolled over on her back to have her tummy rubbed. Beryl scratched her ears and under her pink collar. She pulled her hand away abruptly, involuntarily, as though she'd received a shock. Her cat didn't wear a collar, hadn't since she had become an indoor cat several years ago.

Jude sat up straight, looking regal and proud; she liked her new accessory.

Beryl couldn't catch a breath. Who had done this? Fumbling with the collar she got it off and threw it into a cherry bush. Then she snatched it back, holding onto Jude all the while, so tightly that the cat squirmed and cried. Beryl ran the rest of the way home and retrieved her key from its new spot in the garage. She placed her now panic-stricken pet indoors while she thought about what to do with the collar.

It wouldn't do to have it in the house, but she didn't want to leave it outside for the lunatic that was tormenting her to find and dispose of; it might be evidence. Beryl burst into tears when she imagined herself reporting this new crime to the police. It equaled the deadheading of her lobelia in absurdity: Yes, hello, I'd like to report the fact that an attractive pink collar has been fastened around my cat's neck. Oh, and she seems very fond of it.

This guy, whoever the fuck he was, knew what he was doing.

Beryl stuffed the collar down inside a window well on the north side of the house. Then she covered it with rocks. It wasn't a secure hiding place but it would have to do. She didn't want it in her house.

Then she put her key in her pocket. No more leaving it outside if there was a maniac in her life.

No one was home next door on the north side; that was where Clive Boucher lived and he was never around. He lived on his own, in a house that had been in his family for years. It had fallen to him when he was the only one left to inherit it.

Clive was in a band that had been quite famous in the sixties and early seventies. It was called Crimson Soul. Even after all these years it was still very much in demand for fairs and exhibitions. For all the time Clive spent in the house he may as well rent it out, Beryl thought. But then she'd see him even less and she supposed she'd miss his scruffy presence if he disappeared completely.

His house was a mess, from the outside, anyway. The paint was so old it was hard to tell what colour it was supposed to be. Maybe a beige sort of colour that now looked pretty much like nothing. As close as you could get to the colour of nothing. And peeling badly at that, leaving the worn grey wood at the mercy of the elements. Unlike Beryl's house, which was stucco like most of the others in the area, Clive's house was made of wood.

His house was older than hers, too. It was probably here way back when this part of the Norwood Flats was a golf course. Maybe it was where the greenskeeper had lived. Maybe Clive's long-dead relatives had been greenskeepers.

She knocked on the door of her other next-door neighbours, the Kruck-Boulbrias, on the south side. No one was home there either, which wasn't surprising. It was only four o'clock on a weekday and both of them were teachers at Red River College.

Beryl wasn't sure if it was just Ariadne who went by Kruck-Boulbria or if Mort had also adopted the name. Maybe he was just Boulbria. She wondered if Ariadne Kruck-Boulbria's students made fun of her because of her name. She hoped so.

As she stood knocking, Beryl realized that she largely disapproved of these neighbours because of their behaviour with squirrels. Ariadne couldn't help her fear of the noisy little critters. With all my crazy fears, Beryl thought, I should try harder to give my neighbours a break. I barely know them at all.

And as for the people two doors down on the south side, she didn't even know their names. Things were vastly different from when she was a kid and knew the first and last names of everyone of her street, all their children's names and ages and the names of all their pets. Everyone had kids in those days, so you were more likely to be in and out of their houses. And everyone had a dog, too, that ran free. Now even the cats were chained. No wonder the crows were taking over!

Beryl thought about the black bird that had landed at her feet a few days ago. She had taken it to the river, eased it onto her gardening shovel and carried it down. She didn't want to picture it resting in the bottom of her garbage can, so she took it clear away. After dark, so no one would see her performing the sinister task.

Someone did see her, though, a man out walking his dog. And she had to explain herself or felt she did and he looked at her askance. She wanted to throw the bird at his head and run away. Why couldn't he have been nice to her? His dog even hung back. She had thrown it over the cliff off Lyndale Drive Park, not looking to see whether it landed on the bank or in the muddy water. It was gone, no longer her responsibility.

Beryl glanced across the lane and saw Mrs. Frobisher working in her garden. She walked over.

"Hi, Mrs. Frobisher."

"Hello, Beryl. How are you?" She looked up from thinning her carrots and smiled.

Rachel Frobisher was a beautiful old woman that Beryl admired. She was Ukrainian, though you'd never know it from either of her names. She had been a violinist, then a violin teacher for many years, giving lessons in her home. Her hair was a pure white cloud around her face and her cheeks were pink from her exertions.

"Pretty good, I guess," Beryl said. "How are you?"

"A little stiff from all this bending over, but other than that I can't complain. I'm just ready to take a break. May I offer you a drink?" She looked at her watch. "I don't think it's too early for a cocktail."

"Well, why not?" Beryl said.

Mrs. Frobisher shook them up a pair of Manhattans and they sat on her back patio watching the gradual arrivals of the other people who lived on the street. Except for Clive Boucher and the Kruck-Boulbrias, who probably had some kind of extra-curricular activities.

"I wanted to ask you, Mrs. Frobisher, if you've seen anyone in my yard lately who looked like they didn't belong there. Today maybe, or any other day. Last week perhaps?" Beryl couldn't remember the exact day that her lobelia had been deadheaded.

"Please call me Rachel, Beryl. I'd like it much better if you did."

"Okay, Rachel."

"Well, let me think. I know I didn't see anyone today. Except that beautiful little white cat of yours. She dropped over and sat with me awhile."

"Did she?" Beryl spilled several drops of her drink on her shirt. She had tipped her glass before it reached her lips.

"Shoot! You'd think I'd have learned how to drink from a glass by now, wouldn't you?"

Rachel laughed. "Would you like to go inside and try and get it out before it sets?"

"No. It doesn't matter. It's just a post office shirt. This'll sound crazy, I know," Beryl went on, "but you didn't attach a collar to Jude when she was over here visiting, did you?"

Rachel laughed again, this time heartily and she spilled a little of her own drink.

"No, Beryl. No, I didn't, but I did notice the collar. Are you all right, dear? I'm sorry for laughing. It just seems like such an odd question."

"Yeah, I know it is."

Beryl didn't know whether to confide in her or not. Maybe there was a screw loose under those snow white curls and it was Mrs. Frobisher herself wreaking havoc in Beryl's yard.

"Have you seen anyone, Rachel?" she asked. "Anyone around my house besides me? Besides me and Jude?"

"I don't think so, dear." Rachel pondered the question. "Let me just think a minute." Her forehead wrinkled as she looked backward in time, searching for something that would be of help.

"Just the old woman, I guess, and that would have been last week sometime, maybe even the week before, the last time I saw her. Since I stopped working, the days aren't as structured as they were and one week pretty much runs into another. Yes, just Clive's mother. At least I assume that's who she is. She's the only one I've seen, dear."

A silence surrounded Rachel Frobisher's words, like a picture frame. The words hung between the two women in the clear air.

"Clive's mother?" A coolness flowed down over Beryl's face. She pictured Gatorade running over the coach's head when the Blue Bombers won an important game. It was like that. Only this was in slow motion and it turned warm very quickly.

"Yes," Rachel said. "Does she do some gardening for you?"

"Clive doesn't have a mother," Beryl said.

"Oh?" Rachel looked shaken. "I see her there in his yard. Who is she? An aunt? I...I just assumed..."

"I don't know who she is, Rachel. I've never even seen her. But I have a feeling that she isn't anyone, I mean, anyone that's supposed to be there. Anyone Clive knows."

"What do you mean, Beryl?"

"I don't know for sure."

This bright new knowledge spun around inside Beryl's head till she felt dizzy and very tired. She didn't want it, any of it. She wanted to go home and lie under a blanket on the couch.

"What did this person look like?" she asked in a flat voice, placing her drink on the ground beside her chair. She didn't want it, either. It was too sweet, sickly sweet. It reminded her of the wine she and her friends used to get their hands on when they were teenagers. Wine with names like Prince of Denmark. They'd drink and then sometimes they'd barf.

"Let me see," Rachel said now. "The woman was tall and slim, I know that much."

"Who isn't?" Beryl muttered.

"Pardon?"

"Nothing, Rachel. Go on. Please."

"I didn't see her up close."

Rachel looked as if she was struggling with a picture inside her head. "I'm sure I'll see her again soon, so I'll pay better attention and give you a full report. Maybe I'll introduce myself."

"What was she wearing?"

"A dress. She always wears a dress. An old-fashioned flowered one, now that I think of it. And her hair is grey and pulled back in a bun at the base of her neck. Very old-fashioned, as I say." Rachel looked down at her own overalls and fluffed out the cloud of white hair around her face.

Beryl smiled at her. "Not like you."

Rachel smiled back. "She has big feet," she said. "Too big for the rest of her. Or maybe it was just the shoes she was wearing. Clumpy big things. Usually if you see someone of that age in a dress their footwear goes along with it. You know, ladylike. Not great thunderous shoes."

"Thunderous?" Beryl hoped that Rachel wasn't creating someone just to please her. She didn't doubt that there had been an old woman. But she didn't know Rachel well enough to know if she was remembering a picture of her or creating one.

*Chapter 21*

He likes packing the eye holes with dirt, but not as much as doing the mouth. He doesn't like the part where he has to cut the eyes out, but they seem to be the logical next hole. He's glad he brought the Ziploc bags; they're good for eyes, as well as for his gloves and miniature cultivator. That's what his Aunt Hortense used to call it. He calls it his gouger. His cargo pants have lots of pockets, the kind with flaps and fasteners, so he puts one item in each of his pockets.

The trouble is, one of the eyes collapses when his leg presses against a hefty woman on the bus on his way home. It's rush hour and they're packed together like sardines. She smells like a sardine too; she grosses him out. Luckily it's a short ride to his home stop. He worries on the bus with the eyes in his pockets; he feels conspicuous, hopes nothing leaks or shows in other ways.

He can't save the wrecked one. It's a slippery mess, as though he's been carrying a raw egg around all day. Well, not that bad, but not good enough to keep. He flushes it down the toilet. The good one, the firm one, he places in a jar and sets on the mantel.

Another day he catches a different bus. This one takes him to Brookside Cemetery, where he places the jar on the grave of his Auntie Cunt who's been dead for sixteen years. He places her miniature cultivator there too, to let her know she had a part in it.

On a bench in the graveyard he sits and smokes cigarettes as night falls. Even when he's inhaling the smoke, it's not enough. He wants another one, at the same time.

It reminds him of how he used to feel when he tried to be with girls. Even when they cooperated with his tying-up games, it wasn't enough. And he didn't like the look in their eyes when he told them what he wanted them to do, what he needed them for. Too often he saw pity there, sometimes fear. He preferred the fear.

A picture of the tall woman with no eyes rests inside his head. No one saw him in the park. No one has found her yet. She is still alone.

He wonders if anyone saw him in the back yards. Maybe the white-haired bitch. He loved doing Mail Girl's flowers. Beryl Kyte's flowers. It was the most fun he could remember having in a long time. The cat collar wasn't that great. The animal didn't like him at all. Boyo still has a scratch on his hand from the cat. That makes him angry.

## Chapter 22

A week and two days had gone by since Beryl found the pink collar around Jude's neck.

She stared at the front page of the Saturday *Free Press*. Another dead woman had been found, this time in Whittier Park. According to the paper, there were "similarities between this case and the one involving the woman found in St. Vital Park." One of the similarities was that both victims were very tall, approaching six feet. They published this as a warning to tall women, just in case it was a pattern.

Beryl wondered what the other similarities were and knew that one of them would be connected to the dirt—the dirt that had been packed into Beatrice Fontaine's mouth—that had welcomed the mushroom spores and encouraged their growth.

As she sat on her deck drinking coffee, pondering all this, she realized she was shaking. It was true. When she was too dopey to realize that something was upsetting her, her body let her know about it in one way or another. Someone had told her once that we can't have a single solitary thought in our heads without our bodies reacting in some way. It was comforting in a way, kind of like having a really helpful and clever friend. Beryl remembered shaking when her dad died, shaking when her mum died, but crying on neither occasion.

A tall, slouching figure shuffled slowly down the sidewalk towards her. It was Wally. It was the first time she had seen him since the folk festival.

"Hi, Wally," she said, as he cut across her bumpy lawn. "This is a surprise. What brings you to this neck of the woods?"

Beryl was uncomfortable that he had shown up uninvited. He must have put some effort into finding out where she lived and she didn't like that either.

"Hi, Beryl. Nice deck," he said. "I've come to see you, actually. To see what the climate is surrounding my actions."

"What actions? What are you talking about?"

"My behaviour at the folk festival."

He dragged a green plastic chair over to where Beryl sat on her recliner.

"Oh."

Beryl remembered Wally disappearing that night, but she hadn't really thought about it since. Could that be what he meant?

"Would you like some coffee?" she asked.

"Thanks, Beryl. Black is good."

When they were settled in the shade of the Russian willow sipping their coffee, Wally said, "Have Stan and Raylene spoken about it?"

"About what, Wally? You leaving early, you mean, or what exactly?"

"Yeah. Taking off the way I did, without saying goodbye."

Beryl wanted to shout, "No one cares!" But instead, she said, "Stan certainly hasn't mentioned it and I haven't seen Raylene. I think people probably just figured you caught a bus home or met a friend or something."

"I don't have much in the way of friends," Wally said.

"Oh. Well…" Beryl sighed.

"Sorry. I don't want to burden you."

"No. Don't worry. You're not burdening me." Beryl smiled at him. "I don't think this is worth worrying about, Wally."

"Yeah. Sometimes I worry about stupid things."

"So you haven't spoken to Stan or Raylene, then, since the folk festival."

"No."

"If it would make you feel better you could always apologize to them."

"Maybe I could do that—an apology."

"Of course you could, Wally. But be sure to tell them what you're apologizing for because they might not get it if you don't."

Beryl was getting impatient. She wanted Wally gone so she could think about the new dead person, maybe phone the police to see if they would tell her anything, although she was pretty sure they wouldn't.

Wally sipped his coffee, missed his mouth, and spilled two dark brown splotches on his white golf shirt.

Just like me, Beryl thought.

"Shit!" he said.

She hoped he wouldn't want to try to get the coffee stain out. Wally was too strange for her to want him inside her house. She looked at him and she supposed he was looking back, but his eyes didn't really seem to connect. They darted about. Shifty. The opposite of Sergeant Christie, who could kill you with his eyes.

A squirrel picked up the last of the peanuts Beryl had put out and perched on the edge of a big pot of begonias. It scrounged around in the dirt.

"Should that squirrel be doing that?" Wally asked.

Beryl laughed.

The squirrel ran off with the nut.

"I guess he knew we were on to his hiding place," Beryl said. "He wasn't going to risk having you steal his peanut."

Wally missed his mouth again and coffee dribbled down his chin. "Fuck!"

The squirrel returned and crouched beside Beryl, staring up at her.

"That squirrel is freaky," Wally said. "I don't like him."

Beryl laughed again. She noticed her next-door neighbour, Clive, sitting on his crumbling front steps.

"Hey, Clive," she called.

"Hi, Beryl." He waved.

"I'm going to introduce you to my famous next-door neighbour," she said to Wally and stood up. "And then I have to go in, Wally. I have things to do."

She dragged him over to where Clive sat smoking and sniffing on the step.

"I haven't seen you in a while," she said. "Have you been playing out of town?"

"Yeah." Clive grinned and his long face creased like old leather. "We're doin' fairs down south all summer. I just came home for a couple of days between gigs."

"Wally Goately," Beryl said, "meet Clive Boucher, drummer for Crimson Soul. Remember them?"

"Hi, Clive. Yeah, I do, actually. I'm not much into music of any kind, but I remember you all right. I think I even saw you play once back in high school. Would that have been possible?"

Clive laughed, a whiskey laugh that turned into a cough. "Anything's possible, Wally. Goately, is it? I don't think I've heard that one before. What kind of name is that?"

"A jackass name," Wally said.

Beryl wondered if he ever really smiled. He always wore a horrible grimace on his face, as though life was unbearably painful. For Wally, it probably was.

Clive laughed and coughed some more. "Well, it's good to meet you, man."

"So how long are you home for, Clive?" Beryl asked.

"Just till tonight. I'm not sure why I came home at all. My house is such a mess. It just depresses the shit out of me."

"Oh, I'm sure it's not so bad," Beryl said.

They all three looked up at the house, which looked a little crooked, or maybe it was just the steps that made it look that way. They were definitely crooked and crumbling terribly.

"Those steps are downright dangerous," Wally said.

"So did you bring Wally over here just to cheer me up, Beryl, or what?"

She laughed. She wanted to ask Clive about the old lady that Mrs. Frobisher saw in their yards but she didn't want to ask him with Wally there.

A horn blasted from the back lane and Clive stood up.

"There's my ride. Gotta go."

"Oh. You're going out," Beryl said.

"I've got some business to clear up before heading out tonight. See ya later. Nice meeting you, Wally." And Clive was gone.

"Maybe I'll see you later, before you go," Beryl shouted after him. "We can talk," she added to herself.

She was feeling very resentful of Wally's presence. He was in the way. If she didn't get to talk to Clive today, who knew when he'd be back again?

"I have to go in now," Beryl said. "I have to watch *The Rockford Files.*" She didn't care about hurting Wally's feelings.

He took the hint and cut across her lawn to the sidewalk, leaving the way he had come.

"Your grass is bumpy," he called over his shoulder. "That means you've got lots of worms."

Beryl wondered for the first time how he had gotten here: car, bus, on foot?

"Odd duck," she said to herself and climbed the two wide steps back up to her deck.

## Chapter 23

"I must be a really boring person, even deep down," Beryl said. She lay fully clothed on her own bed with her head on Dhani's chest.

He stroked the smooth skin of her upper arm where it poked out from her summer shirt. "Why would you say that, Beryl? I don't think you're boring at all."

"Thanks. I believe that you don't think I'm boring."

One thing Beryl knew by now about Dhani was that he told the truth as he saw it. Lies didn't sit well with him. Not even the kind that were told to make life easier or to keep from hurting someone's feelings. If Dhani thought Beryl was boring he would say so, if asked. He'd hate saying it, but he wouldn't lie. Dhani held back sometimes, he didn't set out to cause pain, but he wouldn't lie.

"It's not just that I don't think so," Dhani said. "It's an actual fact. You're not a boring person."

"I'm not sure that qualifies as a fact, Dhani. It's more of an opinion—one guy's opinion." She buried her face in the soft hair on his chest and inhaled his scent. "Mmmm," she said. "You smell wonderful."

Dhani had taken his shirt off, but he had checked with her first, to make sure it was okay.

"Why do you think you're boring even deep inside?" Dhani asked. "What made you say that?"

Beryl sat up and leaned against the wooden headboard. "I dreamed I moved my bedside table a little to the left."

"Yes?"

"That's it. That's my dream in its entirety. I moved my bedside table a little to the left."

"Your left or its?"

"What?"

"Your left or the bedside table's left?"

"Dhani, that's crazy."

"No, it isn't."

"Yes, it is."

"No, it isn't."

"How isn't it, then?"

When Dhani got through with her, Beryl realized that she had moved the bedside table a little to *its* left in her dream, a little to *her* right. And he convinced her that since she was seeing something from the table's point of view it made her an interesting person as opposed to a boring one. It was good enough for Beryl.

She knew by now that Dhani had had a wife who died. Her name was Maggie and she died eight years ago from pancreatic cancer. Beryl asked him now if he had a picture of Maggie in his wallet. He did.

"May I see it?" Beryl asked.

"Yes, you may," Dhani said. He reached in his pocket for his wallet and spread an assortment of cards around them on the bed. Library card, credit cards, debit card, driver's license, coffee cards, even a St. Leon Gardens' card. Ten dollars worth of produce gets you one tractor mile and a little stamp of cherries in a square. Fifteen tractor miles gets you ten dollars off your next purchase. Beryl had one of those cards herself.

Maggie was lovely, as Beryl knew she would be. Not super model beautiful, but kind, gentle beautiful, with eyes full of fun. She was looking at the photographer as though she had a bone to pick with him, as though he had been teasing her, or maybe taking the picture against her will.

"Did you take the picture?" Beryl asked.

"Yes," Dhani said. "It's not perfect, I guess, but I caught her by surprise, and that's what I wanted to do."

"She's lovely," Beryl said.

"Yes." Dhani began filing his cards away in his wallet.

"She died before the trouble with your toes," Beryl said.

"Yes. They had started bothering me before she got sick, but not to the point where there had been much serious discussion about them."

So far Dhani hadn't removed his liner slippers with their false toes when he took his shoes off at Beryl's door. She hadn't seen his feet yet.

"I'm sorry Maggie wasn't there to see you through your toes." Her eyes filled with tears.

"It's okay. Beryl…it's okay." Dhani put his arms around her and she snuffled quietly into his fragrant chest.

*Chapter 24*

Beryl stood at her kitchen window on Sunday morning and wished that Dhani had stayed the night. She had been afraid to invite him, afraid he would think she was asking too much. So he went off in the wee hours, to his own home. And he went cheerfully. They hadn't fought last night, not about anything.

The phone rang and she made the mistake of picking it up. It was Joe Paine.

"I'm sorry to bother you, Beryl. I…I know I was driving you a bit crazy with all of my calls back when…well, you know."

"No, that's okay, Joe. It's good to hear from you," Beryl said and then regretted it immediately. It was true. The new murder had caused her to think about Joe and she had wondered how he was getting along. But she didn't want to encourage him, even a little bit.

"I was just wondering if you had heard anything about this new woman that they found in Whittier Park," Joe said.

"Just what I read in the paper," Beryl replied. "Why? Do you know anything else about it?"

"No."

Joe didn't have anything to say. He just wanted to talk about the murders in vague terms and Beryl couldn't blame him. It was just that she didn't want to be the one he was talking to, although she did realize she was the logical choice for him.

"Are you having trouble with this, Joe, with what you saw back in June?"

There was silence on the line for a few seconds and then he said, "Yeah. I guess I am."

He sounded so meek and afraid that again, Beryl had trouble relating this man to the confident, well-liked veterinarian and author of *Doggie Dog Days*.

"Joe?"

"Yes?"

"I think it would probably be a good idea for you to seek some help, someone to talk to who isn't me."

Beryl opened her desk drawer and the face of the mushroom girl stared up at her.

"I don't think I'm that great of a choice for you." Her voice caught in her throat.

She turned the picture over and closed the drawer. "There's probably even support groups for things like this."

"Are you going to join one?" Joe asked.

"No."

"Are you doing okay, then?"

"I think so, yeah." Beryl didn't know if this was true.

There was a long pause then and she walked into the living room. She was sticking her finger into flower pots to see if any of her plants needed water when something occurred to her.

"Joe?"

"Yeah?"

"Has anything odd happened around your house and yard since the mushroom girl, I mean, since Beatrice Fontaine?"

"What do you mean, Beryl?" Joe sounded even more uneasy than he had before.

"I don't know, have you noticed anything odd around your place since June, that made you think maybe someone had been hanging about?"

"Like what kind of thing? Give me an example."

"Vague stuff, but things you would notice."

Beryl didn't want to give him an example. She already regretted bringing it up. She didn't want to talk about the lobelia or the beautiful white cat who was rubbing up against her ankles right now. If anything had happened at Joe's place like what she had tried to describe, he would know what she was talking about. Unless he was totally thick and she didn't think he was. Just frightened and horribly unappealing.

After she got off the phone Beryl decided to ask Stan if he had been to the vet lately and if he had, if Joe Paine had seemed his usual self.

She wondered for a moment if Joe was the person who had violated her yard and cat. His renowned way with animals would have made it possible for him to approach Jude and attach a collar around her neck.

So often, though, she had heard about people who commit heinous crimes starting out on animals. And Joe couldn't be one of those guys—he loved animals.

Not that deadheading lobelia could be considered heinous. It's just that she couldn't stop connecting it in her mind to the two dead women.

And anyway, the person who attached the collar to Jude could very easily have forced himself upon her. Jude was easy.

Beryl lay down on the couch and her sturdy little cat jumped up on her chest and settled in.

"If only you could talk," Beryl said as she gently rubbed Jude's ears. "I wonder what you'd have to tell me."

# Chapter 25

"Hello. We've never actually been introduced, but I see you all the time. My name is Beryl Kyte."

She held out her hand and Frank took it. They stood over the yellow beans at St. Leon Gardens.

He smiled. A weary smile, one that couldn't rid his forehead of deeply etched worry lines. "Hi, Beryl. Yeah, I guess it is about time we spoke. I'm Frank Foote."

"Yes. Hi, Frank. Someone at your house must really like beans."

One bag was full and he was working on another.

He laughed. "Yeah. It seems to be one of the few things we can all agree on—yellow beans with butter and salt and pepper."

"Mmm," Beryl said. "My mouth's watering just thinking about it."

She added more beans to her own bag.

Frank offered her a ride home, which was what she had been hoping for. She had bought more vegetables than she could comfortably carry. And there was the matter of the new dead woman.

As they stood in line to pay for their vegetables, Beryl saw her young neighbour, Russell, and his father over by the ears of corn.

"I'll be in the play area!" Russell called up to his dad and began to make his way over to a cordoned-off section of sand and play structures.

"What?" Russell's dad asked.

"I'll be over here in the play area!" Russell shouted, a little impatient.

"Yes, all right, son, I won't be long." The dad seemed a little surprised by Russell's decisive words and behaviour.

"Hi, Russell!" Beryl called out and waved.

His face lit up. "Hi, Beryl!" he yelled and slid down the slide.

Beryl waved at the dad too. She had never met him, just seen him around, as she had Frank.

"I saw in the paper that there was another body found," she said, as she and Frank settled into his car. She fastened her seat belt, pretending it was second nature to her. It felt a little bit exciting, knowing a cop this way.

"Yes." Frank pulled out onto St. Mary's Road, drove a couple of blocks to Lyndale, where he turned left, and then cruised slowly down the drive toward Beryl's place.

He looked at her. "How are you doing, Beryl? I mean, as regards that business in St. Vital Park. It must've shaken you up some, to have found her, I mean."

"You recognize me from that day, then? I wasn't sure if you did."

"From that day, from the miserable evening when I belted Menno Maersk, from seeing you walking around the neighbourhood. I see you all the time."

Frank turned down her street. "See, I even know where you live."

"This would be creeping me out," Beryl said, "if I didn't also know where you live and how many children you have and your dog's name."

Frank laughed. "This neighbourhood is a bit like a small town, isn't it?"

"Would you be able to tell me what it is about the new person they found that makes her case similar to Beatrice Fontaine's?" Beryl asked.

"She's tall and slim."

"Yeah, they said that in the paper. Anything else?"

"They were both killed where they were found and we think they were both killed in broad daylight."

"How do you know that? The second part, I mean, that they were killed in the daytime?"

"We don't. We just think it."

"Why do you think it?"

Frank stopped the car behind Beryl's house and put it in neutral.

"I shouldn't be talking to you about this."

Beryl stared straight ahead. "I can't stop thinking about the dirt in Beatrice's mouth. About the mushrooms that grew there."

Frank put the car in park.

Beryl undid her seat belt and turned to face him. "Did the new dead person have dirt in her mouth too?"

She stared at Frank's quiet profile. "Were there mushrooms?"

"No."

"No what?"

"No she didn't and no there weren't." Frank turned off the ignition and turned to face Beryl.

"I can't be talking to you about this. I'm so sorry you're having a hard time. No one should have to see something like that. We have something called the VSU downtown, the Victim Services Unit. Why don't I give you their phone number? Someone from the unit would be happy to talk to you about all of this stuff. It's what they're there for."

It was an old car Frank was driving, Beryl noticed, old enough that the front seat was all one, the kind where you could slide over and sit next to the driver and he could put his arm around you. And you could rest your head in his lap while he drove. And feel him get hard against your ear. You could touch him through his jeans and unzip him and take him into your mouth. He would have to pull over to prevent killing you both.

"I like your car, Frank."

Beryl knew she was blushing but there was no way in the world he could know why. If he noticed at all he could think she was having a stroke or something.

"Thanks." He smiled. "But you're not going to flatter any information out of me." He scribbled a phone number and the initials VSU on a small slip of paper and handed it to Beryl.

"May I smoke in your car?" she asked.

"No! Are you crazy? My kids would kill me. They'd think it was me and I'd never be able to convince them otherwise. I smoked for a few months about a year ago and it really freaked them. They figured for sure I was going to die on account of it. So I quit, but they keep a real eagle eye out for any slip-ups."

"Why did you start smoking?" Beryl asked. "Was it a relapse? Did you used to smoke?"

"No. It was my first time. I guess I just wanted to do something different. Don't you ever just want to do something different?"

"Yeah. All the time. Smoking just seems like kind of a stupid thing to have picked."

Frank chuckled. "Yeah. I'm not very imaginative. But, hey, you're a fine one to talk."

"Yeah, I guess. Would you like to sit on my deck so I can smoke?" Beryl asked.

She opened beers for them and they drank to the lives of the two people who had died.

Frank swallowed half his beer in one go.

"There was dirt," he said, "but not in her mouth this time."

Beryl's beer suddenly tasted like dirty coins in her mouth, like she was sucking on old pennies. "Where, then?"

"I don't want to tell you, Beryl."

"Please."

Frank stood up and walked around on the deck. Then he came back and sat down.

"It was her eyes. Someone had gouged out her eyes and filled the sockets with dirt."

"Oh my God," Beryl said. She put her drink down and pressed the palms of her hands against her own eyes and stayed that way for a long time.

"Who found her?" she asked finally and Frank didn't answer. He looked past her, into the branches of the willow tree. Many of its leaves were dying; something was eating away at it, aphids, most likely. But Frank wasn't seeing that; he was miles away.

"Was there anything growing there, Frank, in her eyes?" Beryl pressed on. "Had she been there long enough?"

"What? God! Why does that matter? Why is it of interest to you?"

"I don't know. It just is," Beryl said. "I'm sorry."

She started to cry. Her shoulders shook and her mouth opened in a soft rectangle and tears streamed down her face. She didn't wail, just gasped for breath from time to time. She wasn't sure she was ever going to be able to stop.

Frank crouched by her chair and his knees cracked. He took both of her hands in his and offered her his handkerchief.

Beryl blew her nose.

"I'm sorry," they both said at once and Beryl's chest heaved.

"God, I'm so sorry, Frank. I don't usually cry. Really."

"Crying's okay," he said.

"Thanks." She hiccuped. "And I'm sorry about my terrible questions."

Frank stood up again and stepped down the wide stairs into the yard. He peered at the deck's underside.

"This is very fine workmanship," he said. "Who built it?"

Beryl ignored his question. "Frank, do they have any idea who killed those people?"

He came back up and sat down across from Beryl in one of her green chairs.

"They know a few things," he said, "like that he's left-handed and what sort of tool he used to do the gouging, but they don't have a clue who he is. They figure he used one of those little arrow-shaped devices that people dig around in their house-plants with. But they haven't found it. There's some talk of getting someone in from the RCMP to do a profile of a person they figure would do something like this."

"Will that do any good?" Beryl wiped her eyes and stuffed Frank's handkerchief in her pocket.

"I don't know," he said. "I don't really think that kind of thing helps us much. They'll describe a wack job whose Uncle Cletus tortured him since babyhood and who probably has the outward appearance of a regular guy living a normal life.

"Then we'll catch him," he went on. "But it'll be by our regular-type methods. And it'll turn out that he fits the profile and so what?"

Frank stood up. "I've got to get home," he said. "There are three hungry kids there waiting for their yellow beans."

Beryl had heard that Frank and his wife had separated for a while and she wondered now if they were still apart.

She wanted to tell him about the way a stranger had entered her yard and tended to her flowers when she wasn't home. She was reminded of it by his talk of house plants and arrow-shaped devices. It hung over her like a black veil and she was beginning to feel as though it may not be too silly to mention.

"Thanks for the ride." She followed him to his car.

When he was settled behind the wheel she stuck her head in the passenger window.

"Was there anything, Frank? Growing in her eyes?" Beryl wondered why she couldn't shut up about it. She hadn't even known she was going to say it. She wanted to rip out her own tongue and throw it in the river.

Frank sighed. "Jesus."

He looked at her and then stared straight ahead down the lane.

Russell and his father pulled into their driveway two doors down, on the other side of Clive's place. Beryl wondered if maybe she should ask Russell's dad if he had observed anything weird going on around Clive's yard, or hers.

"I'll give you a hand," Russell announced and took one of the bags from his dad.

"Thanks, Russ. You're quite a help."

"Hi, Beryl!" Russell hollered.

"Hello, Russell!" she shouted back and tried to smile.

A soft breeze stirred the leaves in the Kruck-Boulbrias' Manitoba maple.

"The beginnings of Chinese elms were growing there where her eyes were supposed to be," Frank said. "I shouldn't be telling you this and you're going to wish I hadn't."

He fired up the Dodge.

Beryl knew all about Chinese elm trees. They were the main weed growing in her garden. Clive had a Chinese elm in his yard and the seeds took over in early summer. Those and maple seeds; they were everywhere. Beryl wondered if she would ever be able to weed her garden again without seeing a terrible picture in her head. She'd see it forever; she would never be finished with it.

And she knew that Frank was right; already, she wished he hadn't told her.

As he drove off, she looked after him. He didn't return her wave, even though she was sure he was watching her in his rear-view mirror. Beryl shoved her hands deep into her pockets, where she found Frank's balled-up handkerchief. She didn't want him to dislike her; but it was too late. She had the feeling that at the very least, she creeped him out.

She had planned to work around the yard today but changed her mind without realizing it. She was in her house with the doors closed against the fine summer afternoon before she stopped to think about what she was going to do next. The day got away on her.

Covered in her eiderdown quilt and her two cats, who liked her no matter what, she napped on the couch. In spite of the heat, she felt chilled to the bone.

When Beryl awoke she realized she had forgotten to ask Frank how the women had died, if they had both been killed by the same method, and a million other questions. Not that he would have answered them. She sighed. The questions didn't seem so important now. More details weren't what she needed.

Should she have mentioned that Beatrice was a customer of Hermione's? Would Frank think that was important? There was a lot to keep track of. She doubted she'd make a good police detective.

Frank hadn't mentioned the photograph she had taken from Sergeant Christie's bulletin board. Maybe the sarge hadn't ratted her out, although that seemed hard to imagine.

If I had a party, Beryl thought, I could invite Frank and his wife if he still has one, and the man who built my deck, so Frank and he could talk about the deck and how fine it is.

A late afternoon sunbeam lay across the three of them there on the couch and Beryl felt guilty for sleeping away part of Sunday.

"I don't think I'll be having a party any time soon," she said to her cats as she gently moved out from under them.

She got up and warily opened the back door. There was no immediate evidence of anything dreadful happening outside. Maybe she could convince Clive to have his Chinese elm chopped down. He likely didn't even know he had one. She could chop it down herself when he was out of town. He probably wouldn't notice.

## Chapter 26

"Could you drop by the shop after you finish your route today?" Hermione asked.

It was the first time she had ever phoned Beryl at work. She had managed to get put through to the head office supervisor's desk and Ed shouted Beryl's name out at the top of his lungs.

She made her way to his desk amid much hooting and carrying on from her fellow workers. Any excuse to let off a little steam.

"What's up, Herm?" she asked, breathless. She was always breathless at work. There was never enough time for her to get her mail sorted up satisfactorily.

"I'd rather not talk about it on the phone," Hermione said, "but I'm pretty sure it's important." She didn't like phones any better than Beryl did. "There are two things, actually, and I'm starting to feel that they're connected."

"Could you give me a hint?" Beryl asked.

She could barely hear her friend with all the clanging and banging going on around her at the post office. There was an added high-pitched whir this morning, coming from overhead. It wouldn't let up. The skin on Beryl's face felt too tight for the bone structure underneath and her eyes ached with the sound.

Plus, one of her fellow letter carriers was throwing a fit.

Apparently, one of the people on his route had phoned in to say she was pretty sure she'd seen him throwing something into the Assiniboine River and she wondered if it might be mail. She had been expecting a letter from her cousin in Medicine Hat for a couple of weeks now and was worried that it might have been in the ill-fated bundle.

The letter carrier in question was shouting. "I haven't been anywhere near the river! I haven't thrown anything anywhere! And you can tell that douche bag to stick her head up her own ass! I'm so fuckin' sick of being blamed for things I didn't do! Don't tell me. I bet I can guess who it was. It was old lady Griswold, wasn't it?"

"I've got to go, Herm," Beryl said. "I'll be over as soon as I'm finished work."

She hung up and stood around with the others to watch.

Ed looked at the piece of paper he was holding and said, "Yes, it is Mrs. Griswold who made the complaint."

"Christ, Ed!" said Jeff, the carrier who was throwing the fit. "You know she's a nut job. Why the motherfuck do you even bother me with this crap? I'm going home. I'm sick. I don't know when I'm coming back."

He was out the door before anyone could stop him.

"It's probably just as well," Ed said. "He needs a chance to cool down. Okay, let's get back to work. Any offers to sort up Jeff's mail for him?"

Beryl hurried back to her desk. She wanted to make short work of her route today and find out what Hermione had to say. With three sets of heavy flyers she doubted she'd be making very good time, but at least the weather was good. Sunny and comfortable; the heat had let up some.

By the time she got to the shop it was late afternoon. Hermione was leaning on her desk staring into the middle distance.

"Diane Caldwell was also a customer of mine," she said.

"Who's Diane Caldwell?"

Hermione showed Beryl the *Free Press*. A short article on page three revealed the identity of the second murder victim. Beryl sat down heavily in one of the easy chairs.

"We have to tell the police, Herm. It's too much of a coincidence."

"Yes, I know. I just thought I'd talk to you first because you were saying that one of the cops was nice. Maybe he could be the one I talk to. I don't want to talk to any nasty cops."

"Good idea. I'll phone Frank. He's really great. He doesn't think much of me, but he'll be nice to you for sure. I don't think he could not be nice, unless he was dealing with a really nasty person."

"Why doesn't he think much of you?"

"Because I'm a stupid…twisted…wiener," Beryl said. "You said there were two things you wanted to tell me. What's the other one?"

"Something else happened."

"What?"

"Someone tried to wreck my geraniums." Tears welled up in her eyes and one or two spilled over.

"Oh, Herm."

Beryl looked around her at the lush growth in the clay pots and outside at the window boxes overflowing with healthy plants.

"No, those ones are okay. It's the ones hanging on the stairway up to my flat. They were smashed down on the ground."

"Oh, my God. When did this happen?" Beryl asked. "Did you hear anything?"

"In the night, I guess. I slept really well last night. Of all the nights to have a good sleep!"

Hermione opened her desk cupboard and got out the bourbon.

"I found them when I got up this morning. They were strewn all over the cement down below."

She poured herself a long drink and one for Beryl too.

"I saved all but one of the ones that were left," she said, "replanted them right away in new pots and brought them inside.

I put them in the kitchen window. They should be safe there. Do ya think?"

"What do you mean, of the ones that were left?" Beryl asked.

"Some of them were gone. Not the pots, just the plants."

"That's very weird."

"Yes."

"Maybe you shouldn't have touched anything," Beryl said.

"I couldn't just leave them." Tears ran down Hermione's face. This was the first time Beryl had seen her cry and it frightened her a little.

"I'm so sorry, Herm."

"I left the pots," Hermione said. "I just touched dirt and plants." She wiped her eyes with her sleeve. "My good-natured little geraniums didn't deserve this."

Beryl got up and put her arm around her friend's shoulders for a moment. Skin and bones. Didn't anyone eat anymore?

"I didn't think it was anything more than just horrible children at first." Hermione sniffed. She hauled out a huge white handkerchief and blew her nose, a great honking sound.

"Then when I read the paper, I started thinking it might be connected to me personally and not just be random assholedness. I thought the geraniums and Diane and Beatrice might all be part of the same thing."

She looked at Beryl. "Do you think I'm being paranoid?"

"No, I don't." Beryl told Hermione about the deadheading of her lobelia and Jude's pink collar and her own uneasiness. Then she said, "Let's phone Frank."

She remembered that she had his handkerchief, freshly laundered and even ironed in a kitchen drawer. She wasn't sure how to go about giving it back to him, but she didn't want him to think that she planned to keep it.

After talking to three separate people, Beryl finally heard the now-familiar voice, the one she wanted, the one that would help to make everything okay.

"Frank Foote speaking."

# Chapter 27

The next day Beryl stopped by Hermione's shop again on her way home from work. She found her out back. There was an old moss-covered picnic table set up as a sort of work station, and Hermione was puttering around with cuttings from plants, setting them up in shallow sandy pots till they took root and she could plant them anew.

Beryl sat for a few minutes with her feet up and watched.

"Go inside and get yourself something to drink if you like," Herm said.

"No, I'm good, thanks. I won't stay. I just wanted to see how you were getting along."

Hermione smiled. "Fine. Good."

"It was me who talked you into putting your geraniums outside," Beryl said.

"Don't even start, Beryl. This is not your fault."

"But if I had just kept my big—"

"Ssh! I mean it!"

"But I—"

"Ssh!"

Beryl laughed. "Okay. So how did you like Frank?"

She had gone home yesterday after reaching Frank on the phone. He said he would drop by Hermione's shop and Beryl didn't want to muddy up the situation by being there when he arrived.

"Yeah, he was really nice, just like you said." Hermione scratched her nose with the back of her hand but got sand on her face anyway.

"I don't know how seriously he took the flower pot smashing, but he was pretty concerned about both women being customers of mine."

"Yeah. That's good. It should be taken seriously. They were both shaped like you too, Herm, tall and thin. Shouldn't you be careful?"

"Frank certainly seems to think so. But what am I supposed to do? Hide?"

"Maybe. You could come and stay at my house for a while."

"Beryl, there's strange stuff going on at your house too! You should be being careful too!"

"But my stuff doesn't seem vicious like this and I'm not tall and thin. This tall thin business worries me."

"Yeah, but you are a customer of mine and you're certainly not short and fat."

"No. I'm medium." Beryl stood up. "Anyway, I have to go home and soak my feet."

"They were strangled," Hermione said. "Frank said the women were strangled with scarves."

Beryl sat down again, while her friend told her everything that Frank had described to her about the way the women had died.

"I guess it's not really secret information, if he told you about it," Beryl said. "But it wasn't in the paper." She wished Frank had told her more. She was jealous of Hermione's knowledge.

"No, but I wouldn't go blabbing it. I think that's the type of thing they don't put in the paper because of false confessions and copycat crimes and things like that."

"I won't go blabbing! I wonder why he told you and not me."

"He didn't mean to, I'm pretty sure. It was just sort of out there before he knew it. I think your Frank is a wee bit troubled. Or preoccupied, anyway."

"He's not my Frank," Beryl stood up again and fastened on her mail bag. "And I won't go blabbing," she added quietly.

"How's your new bag working out?" Herm asked.

"Good. It makes all the difference in the world," Beryl said sadly.

She stepped out onto the sidewalk in front of Hermione's shop and saw Wally standing across the street staring at her. He waited for a break in the traffic and crossed the road.

"You'd think geraniums were the only flower in the world," he said in that hard-done-by way of his, as he took in the window boxes and gigantic flower pots.

"What have you got against geraniums?" Beryl asked. "I think they're beautiful."

"She's a weirdo, ya know," Wally said, gesturing with his head in the direction of Hermione's shop. "Why do you hang around with her?"

"What kind of a thing is that to say?" Beryl stared. "You're way weirder than she is, Wally. Way weirder. How do you know Hermione, anyway?"

"Is that her name? That figures. I don't know her. I've just seen her."

Beryl started walking and Wally followed along.

"She's a lesbian, you know," he said.

"So what? You're an ignorant simpleton. What are you doing around here, anyway? Don't you live in some stupid part of town?"

Beryl knew she was behaving terribly, but something in Wally brought out the junior high in her. She wanted to hurt him. Certain by now that she didn't like him, she didn't want to see him here on her turf. Maybe he was the guy smashing pots of geraniums and killing people.

"Really, what are you doing here, Wally?"

"Gettin' my hair cut," he said. "No, not with her," he added when Beryl's eyes opened wide in disbelief. "I go to Larry, the barber. He's cheap and good and he doesn't make me talk."

Beryl left Wally at the door of Larry's and walked home. Her new bag did make a difference in the way her neck and back felt. Neckwise and backwise it was very good thing.

# Chapter 28

"I don't think I like Wally very much," Beryl said to Stan.

He chuckled. "Beryl, you don't really like anyone very much, do you?"

"Yes, I do," she said. "I really like you. I like Dhani, except he makes me really mad sometimes, I like Frank Foote, I like Hermione a lot…"

"Who's Frank Foote?"

"The policeman."

"Oh, yeah."

"There are lots of people I like," she started to insist. "At least there used to be. I don't know what's happened."

Sometimes Beryl wished she were married to Stan. They got on so well together. He was already married, though.

"I like Raylene," she said quietly.

It was Stan's second marriage. He had a grown daughter from the first, whose ass he thought the sun shone out of. Of course, Stan thought the sun shone out of everyone's ass. That was perhaps the thing Beryl liked best about him. Maybe she could learn it from him.

He was walking her home. He did this sometimes if he'd had a good day and wasn't too tired. He lived in Norwood too, on the other side of St. Mary's Road. In the sticks. At least that's what people had called it when Beryl was a kid: the sticks, where Stan lived and the flats, where she lived. Lived both then and now; they had both moved to Norwood as small children and neither of them had travelled very far.

Beryl watched withered leaves skittering down the boulevard. The day before, in a high wind, they had blown from some of the trees that the aphids had struck. One of those trees was in Beryl's yard, her willow. She worried about its health; if it was in good shape, why wasn't it doing a better job of fighting off the aphids?

Silence screamed down the length of the lane. She wondered for a moment if she had gone deaf. Shouldn't she be able to hear the dry familiar rustle of fallen leaves as they swept along the boulevard?

"Stan?"

"Yes?"

"Nothing. It's just so quiet. I wanted to hear a sound."

"Yeah, it's strange, isn't it?" Stan said. "It's like we're the only two people on earth. Did you ever see that episode of *The Twilight Zone* where there was only the one man left in the world after a nuclear explosion, but he came to terms with it because he discovered he was sitting on the steps of an undamaged library? And he loved to read?"

"Shh!" Did you hear that?"

"What?"

"I don't know. You were talking. It sounded like a groan. Or a moan maybe."

They had almost reached Beryl's house by now and they stopped and listened to the quiet.

"I don't hear anything," Stan said.

"Shh!"

A breeze swirled dry leaves around the bottoms of their hideous postal pants and Beryl could hear them now. But it wasn't until they entered her back yard that she heard another moan.

"There," she whispered. "Did you hear it?"

"Yes, actually. I did," Stan said. "It sounds like it's coming from Clive's yard."

"Is that you, Beryl?" Clive's voice called over the low cedar fence.

"Yes it is, Clive. Is everything all right over there?"

"Very much so, thanks."

Clive's long, deeply lined face appeared above the fence like a misshapen jack-o'-lantern.

"Candy, meet my neighbour, Beryl Kyte, and Stan Socz. They're mailmen."

A face appeared next to Clive's, only higher up. Beryl realized now that the moans she had heard were connected to this pair's sexual shenanigans and she started to suspect they were naked on the other side of the fence.

They were both kneeling, but even so, Beryl could tell that Candy was very tall. She thought about the tall woman that Mrs. Frobisher had reported seeing in their yards. But that woman had been old. Candy was young. And a hooker. All Clive's girlfriends were young hookers and they were also all tall. He requested tall, long legged.

He had told Beryl that one night when she hadn't been able to sleep. He'd joined her on her deck with a bottle of tequila and they'd decided to share a secret, one each. That had been his.

Beryl's was that she'd eaten eleven doughnuts once, back in 1983. All on the same day. She'd flushed the twelfth one down the toilet after breaking it into small pieces.

"Weren't you out of town, Clive?" she said now. "I'm surprised to see you."

"Yeah, I was. I just got back last night."

Beryl had been wanting to speak to Clive, ever since the day she talked to Rachel Frobisher, to ask about the tall old lady and other things, like if he'd noticed anything unusual at all around his home, but she didn't suppose now was the time.

So all she said was, "Did you find everything at your house as it should be?"

"Hmm, I think so. Shouldn't it be as it should be?"

"Well, yeah, I guess. Anyway, nice seeing you, Clive. And you Candy. We have to go."

Beryl didn't want to see either of them naked. She looked at Stan and saw that he wouldn't have been in agreement with her over this. He would have liked very much to see Candy naked, though probably not Clive. She gave him a little push.

"See ya, Clive," Stan said. "Nice meeting you, Candy."

"Later," Clive replied.

Candy didn't speak. Maybe speaking wasn't part of the package.

"I wonder if the tall woman Mrs. Frobisher talked about was just one of Clive's prostitutes." Beryl spoke quietly when they had settled themselves on the deck. She didn't know where her neighbour was now, in or out, front or back. And there was also young Russell. He often crept up out of nowhere.

"Hmm, I doubt it," Stan said. "The person she described didn't sound much like a hooker."

"Unless she dressed up like that especially for Clive, like if it's some twisted thing he's got going."

Beryl had told Stan everything by now, so there were three friends that were totally in the picture. Hermione, Stan, and Dhani. Two friends, if you took into account that Dhani didn't know certain things, like that the women were Hermione's customers. Four, if you took into account that Stan had probably confided in Raylene.

"But Clive may well not have even been here," Stan said, "when Mrs. Frobisher saw the old lady."

"Yeah. I just don't know, I mean, when he's here and when he isn't. He just sort of pops up and then disappears again."

"Literally pops up," Stan said, and took a long swallow of his Fort Garry Pale Ale.

"Yeah."

"Your willow tree doesn't look so good." Stan batted at the mosquitoes.

"I know," Beryl said. "I'm just sick about it. What if it dies?" She handed him her mosquito repellent.

"It won't." Stan slathered the lotion on his neck and arms.

"Anyway," he said, "that *Twilight Zone* episode I was telling you about?"

"Yeah?"

"The guy's glasses didn't survive the nuclear disaster and he was blind as a bat without them, so it ended up being a very sad story."

Stan left after one beer and Beryl went inside to shower and change. From her kitchen window she watched Candy leave in a taxi.

After a supper of yellow beans, new potatoes, and chocolate chip cookies she went outside again to fool around in the yard.

There was Clive carrying his recyclables out to the lane.

"Hi, Clive."

"Hey, Beryl. How's it goin'?" He was sweating profusely in spite of the cool evening and his face was grey. But he smiled; Clive always smiled.

Beryl noticed that his newspapers were thrown in with his cans and bottles. Plus, his recyclables stunk. He didn't rinse anything out very well, if at all.

"Do the recycling guys not complain to you about the state of your blue box?" Beryl asked.

"So far, not," Clive said. "Why, what's the matter with it?"

"It stinks."

"Garbage is supposed to stink."

"Recyclables aren't garbage."

Maybe he doesn't understand the principle of recycling, Beryl thought.

"Clive?"

"Yes?"

"Does anyone ever housesit for you?"

"Whaddya mean?"

Clive set his blue box down by the curb and wiped his hands on his jeans.

"I mean, does anybody ever stay in your home when you're out of town?"

She gestured toward his house.

Clive looked at it. "God, what a mess it is," he said.

Beryl followed his gaze.

"I guess it could use a little work here and there."

You could see an actual hole in one corner of the house if you looked closely and that's what Clive was doing now. And there was absolutely no paint left on the trim around the windows and doors.

"I have squirrels in the attic, or something, anyway. I can hear them scrambling around."

"Oh, boy."

"And Beryl?"

"Yes?"

"I saw a mouse in the basement when I was doing the laundry. At least, I hope it was a mouse."

"Good heavens, Clive. Be sure not to mention any of this to the Kruck-Boulbrias."

"Who?"

"The Kruck-Boulbrias. My next-door neighbours on the other side. They'll have you arrested or quarantined or something. You're going to have to do something about some of these things, Clive. Start with the mouse, with the live things. They shouldn't be in your house."

Beryl didn't want mice or rats or whatever they were getting tired of Clive's place and setting their sights on hers. She pictured herself asking Mort Kruck-Boulbria if she could borrow his rodent trap. After her nasty comments to him about squirrels.

"Phone somebody," she said to Clive. "Phone Poulin's. And get someone to patch up the holes there in your foundation and wherever."

"But I'm never here. For instance, I'm going out of town again tomorrow."

"Then give me a key, Clive, and I'll do it."

"Really, Beryl? I don't want to impose."

"It's no trouble, honestly," Beryl said. "At least not compared to the trouble an infestation of giant killer rodents would be."

"Just a sec," Clive said and went into the house.

He came back with a key. It looked like the key that Beryl had worn around her neck when she was a kid. To unlock the big front door of the empty house on Ferndale Avenue.

"This key looks like it was cut to fit the original lock on the original door of this house seventy years ago," she said.

"I guess it probably was."

"Wow. Most people would have new doors by now, Clive, or at least new locks, new keys."

"This one still works, I think." He stuck the key in the old-fashioned lock on the door.

"So, you don't usually lock your doors?"

Beryl was reminded of the reason she had started this conversation in the first place.

"It fits!" he shouted. "Sometimes I do. I mean, I have locked them, at times. There's not a heck of a lot in there to steal. I keep my drums somewhere else. My stereo equipment and stuff isn't exactly state of the art. I'm not sure anyone would want it."

Beryl had thought that a musician would have a really great sound system.

"Don't you listen to music?"

"Not very often."

"That's odd, Clive."

"I don't like anything anymore. The last thing I liked was probably recorded in 1972."

"Well, why don't you listen to that?"

"I'm never here," he said, impatience beginning to creep into his voice.

Beryl could see that she was starting to irritate Clive, so she brought the conversation back to the subject she was really interested in before she lost him again.

"Clive, does anyone ever stay here while you're away?"

"No. Not that I know of. Why?"

"You mean you don't know for sure?"

"Well, it's just that one or two things have seemed out of whack to me on occasion when I've come home…this time for instance."

"What?" Beryl opened Clive's milk shute and a pile of junk mail fell to the ground. "What was out of whack?"

"My bed smelled funny. Like dirt. And…" Clive stopped.

"And what?" She knelt to tidy up the mess.

"Well, there was this funny little newspaper under my bed."

"Funny little newspaper? What do you mean a funny little newspaper?"

"It's a *Pilot Mound Sentinel.*"

Beryl stood up and tried to hand Clive the pile of flyers.

Clive kept his hands in his pockets. "I don't want that shit. What do I want with all that shit?"

"Clive, if you don't want junk mail, you should put up a sign that says so. Your mailman would be glad not to deliver it. A pilot mound sentinel. Is that what you said?"

"Yeah. It's a weekly newspaper from Pilot Mound, Manitoba. That's a town. I've actually been there, believe it or not. Or by it, anyway. I had a gig in Crystal City when I was in another band for a while, way back, in 1966 or something. Crystal City is, like, the next town over. I remember nothing about Pilot Mound other than that it was there."

Beryl dragged a dusty nylon weave lawn chair over and sat down on top of the flyers to keep them from blowing away.

"May I see it, Clive, the newspaper?"

"Sure. Do you want to come in or should I go get it?"

"What the heck. Why don't I come in? Do you realize I've never been in your house?"

"Well, you're not missing much. Come on, then. But excuse the mess. I'm not much of a housekeeper."

Clive grinned sheepishly, but nothing prepared Beryl for what hit her when he opened the door.

Hot rank air enveloped her as she stepped tentatively forwards. She had felt this before. Sometimes, when she knocked on the door of a downtown apartment with a registered letter or priority post the thick foul air knocked her backwards just as it did now. Some people live and breathe inside that air. She hadn't known that Clive was one of them.

How would he even know if his bed smelled like dirt? Clive looked okay outside the house. A little shabby, maybe, and his hair could use a wash. But nothing to warn her of how he lived on the inside.

Beryl didn't want to go in. And she didn't know what to say. She didn't want to make him feel bad. They were in the kitchen now and Clive pulled out a chair from the chrome kitchen set.

"Here, sit down and I'll go find the newspaper. Would you like a drink?"

The chair was sticky and Beryl perched on the very edge. The counter was a mess of filthy glasses and liquor bottles, some empty, some with dregs. At least it was a surface where she could put down the flyers. Beryl noticed a cigarette butt floating in the bottom of a vodka bottle. It had turned the booze a russet colour. She shuddered, remembering a long-ago party, when she had taken a swig from a beer bottle she had thought was hers, and had gotten a mouth full of tobacco and cigarette paper.

"I don't think so, thanks." She wanted a drink rather badly but not out of any of these bottles.

When Clive left the room she opened the fridge, which was surprisingly clean inside and filled with beer.

"Maybe I'll have a beer!" she called after him. She twisted off the top and drank from the bottle.

Clive returned with a thin faded newspaper and handed it to Beryl: The *Pilot Mound Sentinel*. It was a summer date and the year was 1981.

"Did you notice the year on this, Clive?"

He peered over her shoulder. "Well, I'll be fucked!"

"Yeah. This is really old. Did you read it?" Beryl asked as she gently turned a yellow page. There weren't many pages to turn.

"No." Clive opened the fridge and opened a beer for himself.

"Have you thought about phoning the police, Clive, about this newspaper and your bed and everything?"

Clive chuckled. "No way, man. The last thing I need is cops inside my house." His eyes darted about. "Jesus, Beryl. I can't be havin' cops inside my house."

Beryl looked around her, took in the pipes and papers and bags of dope.

"No, I suppose not," she said. "And anyway, the crime is a little vague." Just like my crimes, she thought, picturing her lobelia and the bright pink cat collar. She almost mentioned them to Clive, but decided against it.

"May I borrow this?" she asked, folding up the worn pages.

She didn't know what she was looking for, but she knew there was something in this little newspaper printed so long ago.

"Sure. You can keep it if you like. I don't have a lot of use for a Pilot Mound newspaper from 1981." Clive drained his beer bottle. "Do you?"

"Well it's a clue, isn't it? Clive, aren't you even a little bit interested in who left this, who may have been sleeping in your bed?"

"I don't know. I guess not. So many people are in and out of here, Beryl. It's probably somebody I actually know or have at least met. They probably knew I was out of town and crashed here, figuring it would be okay. Why are you so interested in this?"

Beryl couldn't imagine living the way Clive did. At least not these days. Maybe back in the early eighties around the time when this little newspaper was published, but not now, when doors were double dead-bolted, alarms were set, and window bars were a matter of course. Except at Clive's house.

She decided not to answer his question and he didn't pursue it.

"Do you wanna share a little blow?" Clive was lining up two tidy rows of white powder on the crusty surface of the kitchen table.

"No thanks, Clive. I should be going."

Beryl took a last drink from her beer bottle and set it down amongst the clutter. "I'm going to read this thing cover to cover and see what it tells me."

She didn't want to inhale anything more of Clive's right now, least of all little pieces of grunge from his filthy table mixed in with some questionable cocaine.

"Take care, Clive," she said and left him there, hunched over, with a five dollar bill stuck up his nose.

He gave her the thumbs-up sign but she was out the door before he looked up again.

# Chapter 29

"Fuck!" Boyo pounds the wall with his fist.

His newspaper is gone. He shouldn't have been so careless. Imagine being that careless! It was the only copy he had of Auntie Cunt's obituary.

He remembers the night soon after her death when he sat down to write it. Someone had to, he supposed, and he was the only one. She died in Winnipeg, but he composed a death notice for Pilot Mound too, where she had lived the first thirty-four years of her life. He sent it to the newspaper there, the *Pilot Mound Sentinel*. That way, anyone in that small southwestern town who remembered her could breathe their own sigh of relief.

Hortense croaked, he wrote, and laughed out loud.

Old Hort finally kicked the bucket. He opened a bottle of champagne and changed what he had written.

Finally he decided on: Hortense Frouten died.

He didn't mention himself as her survivor or anything to indicate there had been a person there, where there was no more. She was just a name on paper, before and after.

He much preferred the after.

That night, after he'd finished with Hort's obituary, he headed down to the Low Track for the first time. He came to find that hookers were much easier to deal with than the few girls he'd had a go at. They didn't question him as much or seem to judge him. And if they wouldn't do what he wanted them to, they could line him up with someone who would. They joked sometimes, about his ladies' scarves and other items, and he didn't like that much. But they also knew when to stop. They took him seriously; they understood that it would be very easy for him to pull just a little tighter.

Also, whores expected a little pain, to be on both the receiving and the giving ends of some discomfort. They weren't as likely to get into a lather about it if they were squeezed too hard or if he wanted them to buckle him up a little more tightly than usual. He much preferred them to regular women.

So sometimes he made the trip to the Low Track, but more often he phoned a service that would deliver someone to his house in a taxi. It was slicker that way, less noticeable, except maybe to his neighbours. Also, he could use more of his equipment. He set up a special room for his needs.

In early August of 1981, someone from the *Pilot Mound Sentinel* sent Boyo a copy of the paper that ran Hortense's obituary.

He has carried it with him ever since. Not all the time; but often. And when it isn't travelling with him, it's in a plastic folder on the mantle where he can see it from his chair.

And that's where it isn't right now.

Losing it bothers him very much. He needs it back, or at least another original copy. He can't live without one.

# Chapter 30

Beryl watched Dhani sleep. It was the morning after the first night he had slept over and she wasn't sure yet whether it had been a good idea to let him stay. It would depend a lot on how he behaved when he woke up. She didn't want to fight with him first thing in the morning. It would colour her whole day.

He looked so clean and smooth. He looked healthy—indestructible. She loved the look of him.

She knew the indestructible part was an illusion and that even the healthy part could be. She'd had another friend like that—not like Dhani, no one was like Dhani—but a friend who had shone with life and good health. A pre-Georges boyfriend, named Brian. He had up and died on her. One day he had been laughing his head off on the corner of Portage and Main and the next day he was dead: a blood clot in the brain.

Dhani's eyelids fluttered open and he smiled. Beryl kissed him on the temple and he closed his eyes again.

"I'm going to make us some pancakes this morning," Dhani said and Beryl kissed him gently at the edge of his mouth.

"Mmm," she said. "That's my favourite breakfast."

"I know."

He put his arm around her and she rested her head on his chest. Her feet were touching his feet. They felt fine to her. She had been a little worried about seeing and feeling his feet minus their toes, but it hadn't been scary at all. They both drifted off for a few more minutes. Beryl continue to doze while he got up and prepared the pancakes.

He had kissed the smooth skin on her back last night, softly and all over. It was almost her favourite place to be kissed.

They ate breakfast in bed with the late July sunshine streaming in the south window. Dhani made very good pancakes and he made them from scratch.

"It's a recipe my dad used to make, apparently," he said. "It's better than a mix. At least, I think so."

"I do too," Beryl said. "Every bite was delicious. Did your dad not make them for you, then?"

"If he did, I don't remember. He died when I was just four."

"Oh, I'm sorry." Beryl wanted to know more, but didn't want to ask too much at once.

They sipped their coffee, which was also delicious, albeit a little weaker than what Beryl was used to. It reminded her of their many differences.

"If only we didn't fight all the time," she said.

Dhani sighed in a very contented manner and smiled at her.

"I think it's okay that we fight as much as we do," he said.

"Really?"

"Yes, really."

Jude and her brother, Dusty, had settled in at the end of the bed and were staring at Dhani. This was something new for them.

"Some of our differences are rather great, don't you think?" Beryl said.

"Oh? Like what?"

"Well, like the invisible connections you're always rambling on about…"

"Wait!" Dhani said and set his coffee down on the bedside table. "I get the feeling when you say invisible you mean something totally different from what I would mean by that same word. You mean non-existent, don't you?"

He was accusing her and she knew she deserved it. That was what she'd meant, but she'd thought she could bury it inside the word invisible.

"Yeah, I guess that is what I mean."

"Say what you mean, Beryl."

"I'll try."

"What else?"

"Pardon?"

"The other huge differences between us, besides your disrespect for my ideas about connections. What are they?"

"Uh-oh, I should never have started on this. It can't lead to anything good," Beryl said. "And disrespect isn't right. I don't disrespect anything about you."

"What else?" Dhani asked.

"Well…" Beryl crossed her arms in front of her chest. She had thrown on a tee shirt. "I think you rifling through my kitchen drawers is kind of a big thing."

"I agree that I shouldn't have done that."

"Really?"

"Yes. I'm ashamed of having done that."

"Really?"

"Yes. Really. You say 'really' a lot. Do you know that about you?"

"Dhani, if you realized you were wrong in looking through my drawers, why didn't you apologize?"

He picked up his coffee and took a sip.

"Shame…pride…embarrassment…wanting to forget I ever did it. I don't know. I'm sorry for having done that, Beryl, and I'm sorry I didn't apologize right at the start."

"I totally forgive you," Beryl said, and kissed Dhani's brown shoulder. She loved the way her white skin looked against his darkness. For years she had tried to tan in the summer, but she burned so easily it wasn't worth it.

Dusty and Jude had moved halfway up the bed now and were nestled in between Beryl and Dhani's legs. They still stared at Dhani but both cats were getting heavy-lidded and it wouldn't be long till their heads started to nod and they dropped off to sleep.

"This discussion is a pretty good idea, I think," Beryl said.

"Those are minuscule differences," Dhani said. "Both of them."

Beryl turned to look at him. He meant it.

"Do you really think so?" she asked.

"Yes."

"Well, then, give me an example of what you think a big one would be," she said.

"I don't think we have any what you would label really big differences."

"Really?"

"You make coffee too strong and you say 'really' too much."

"What word would you have me use instead?"

"I don't know."

"Well, let me know if you think of it. I think that you make coffee too weak."

"You know what?" Dhani placed his drained cup back on the table and took hold of one of Beryl's hands.

"What?"

"I don't think I can think of a difference between us that would be bigger than what we could handle," he said. "Go ahead, say it."

"Really?"

"Yes, really." He kissed her forehead. "I'll think about it some more, but unless I find out you have bodies in the basement or something, or you find out I'm an impostor or something, which I'm not, by the way, I can't imagine..."

"If I hadn't seen you before, I may well have thought you were an impostor the first day I met you, when you put my foot in your mouth. A layman impersonating a pharmacist."

Dhani laughed. "You had seen me before?"

"Yup. I had seen you behind your counter. I hoped that you'd be the one to help me on the day I got stung."

"Really?"

"Yup. Really."

Beryl wasn't entirely sure she agreed with Dhani about being able to handle their differences but she was very glad that he thought he could. He even thought that she could. She wondered if he would feel the same way if he knew the secret she was hiding from him: that both the murdered women, Beatrice Fontaine and Diane Caldwell, were customers of her good friend, Hermione—that she, and therefore he, had that added connection to the victims.

"I love that you think we could handle all our differences," she said out loud.

She almost said, I love you. That was what she wanted to say. But she was glad she didn't.

## Chapter 31

After Dhani left, Beryl made a fresh pot of strong coffee and took the little newspaper Clive had given her out to the deck. What had happened in Pilot Mound, Manitoba in the summer of 1981? Behind the bold type, *Pilot Mound Sentinel*, was a drawing of a low mound of earth with a cheerful sun rising up behind it. A happy little town?

She perused the news items on the front page: an introduction to the four new members of the "Division Board"; invitations to sign up for bridge and cribbage tournaments and curling leagues; news from villages in the area, she supposed, with names like Wood Bay and Marringhurst; an announcement about the number of babies born in the whole of Manitoba the previous year, and the number of weddings, and then comparisons to previous years.

Beryl wanted to hop in a time machine and travel back to 1981, to the sunny little town of Pilot Mound, where she could take up with one of the Board Members, the one named Earl Addison, marry him and bear his children. She could join the United Church Women, perhaps be a Unit Leader and organize tea towel showers for the old age home and rummage sales in the church basement. She could bake buns and have a dog that ran free.

Not that the world was innocent in the summer of 1981. Richard Speck and Charlie Manson were old news. Even Canada's own Clifford Olson had done most of his bloody work by then. But still, maybe in a small prairie town, maybe in Pilot Mound, Manitoba, a person could have found a terror free life.

*Dark Night of the Scarecrow* starring Charles Durning and Tonya Crowe had been playing at the Tivoli Theatre.

The drugstore advertised perfumed talc "fresh from England" for only one dollar and thirty-nine cents.

There were two obituaries—also on the front page. One for a man named Wilfred Simpson Harvey, who had lived his entire life in Pilot Mound. Practically a whole column rambled on about his war record and his willingness to lend a hand. His relatives were listed: siblings, wife, children, grandchildren, great-grandchildren. Even one or two life-long friends. A well-loved man.

And then there was Hortense Frouten. Hortense Frouten died, it read, and not much else: her dates, the fact that she spent her latter years in Winnipeg, and that was about it. A feeble effort by the writer to plump it out a little. It must have been done by either someone who didn't know her at all or who didn't like her one bit.

That obituary was the only thing on page one that stood out for Beryl. Not what it said, but what it didn't. The person who wrote this felt they had it right with just this terse announcement. There was nothing more to say.

Hortense Frouten was not a loved woman. Not by the person who wrote her obituary, anyway. Beryl wondered if there might be a longer notice in the *Winnipeg Free Press* and decided to try to find out. Maybe this was just the condensed version for her hometown paper. After all, she had lived the final years of her life in Winnipeg.

Beryl perused the rest of the newspaper: the Horticultural Report, Rebekah notes, CGIT notes, a column called *Along the*

*Farm Front.* There was a classified ad for a well boring service, one for the sale of a cow (a heavy milker), and one with an offer of one hundred pounds of netted gem potatoes for $5.89.

Nothing jumped out at her the way the death of Hortense Frouten did. That was it. The stark obituary was definitely it.

But definitely what? She didn't have a clue. Her gut told her it was something, though. I'll let it sit, she thought, as she drank the last of her coffee. Something will come clear.

*Chapter 32*

On Sunday evening Beryl went for a long walk, all the way over to Old St. Boniface. On her way up Provencher Boulevard she saw Wally entering a fried chicken joint. She considered catching up with him and then thought better of it. So what if he was related to Stan and Raylene? She didn't like him and was pretty sure she never would. And anyway, she was trying to air out her head, get her thoughts in order, decide what to do next, if anything.

She walked all the way to Whittier Park, the site of Diane Caldwell's murder. Strangled with a scarf, so Frank told Hermione. Both of the women. The killer had left the scarf behind on Diane, still tied around her throat. He had left nothing with Beatrice, but Frank said it had been done the same way with the same type of scarf. An old-lady scarf he called it. So Hermione said. They could tell by the fibres left in her neck. Not on her neck. In it.

Beryl shivered. What a horrible way to die. She wondered about the hooker from awhile back, whose murder was still unsolved, wondered if she, too, had been strangled with an old-lady scarf.

Some men were playing baseball in the park. Older guys, some with stomachs sticking out over their waist bands. They wore uniforms—very official looking. She recognized two of the men on the home team: Mort Kruck-Boulbria and Frank Foote. She watched for a little while. Frank saw her and waved. Mort didn't appear to notice her.

As she walked back down Provencher she saw an ambulance outside the restaurant Wally had entered about an hour before. She'd heard the siren while she was watching the ball game. At least she assumed that was the siren she'd heard; lately there seemed to be sirens everywhere. The ambulance attendants weren't hurrying. It must have been a false alarm, or maybe they were too late. They slammed the doors shut and drove off slowly, this time without the siren.

Beryl walked by Cuts Only. Hermione must have gone to bed. The only lights were the tiny white ones lighting up the side stairs. It still looked nice, but kind of empty with no geraniums hanging there.

The big clay pots were still out front. And the overflowing window boxes. It was quite dark, after ten by now, but Beryl was sure there was something not right about the plants. They had a wilted look to them. She felt the earth and it was fine; there was no way these plants were neglected. Maybe she was just imagining it. The flowers were still pretty, the leaves still a deep green, but no, they weren't well. She knew it.

Well, if Herm was sleeping, Beryl certainly wasn't going to wake her up with more bad news. She considered standing sentry outside her friend's shop, or sitting sentry, at least till the sky began to lighten in the east.

But she had to be at work by six in the morning, just eight hours from now. And tomorrow was Monday, the worst. Her shoulders ached just thinking about it. She tried to cheer herself up with thoughts of her new double bag; it didn't work.

## Chapter 33

*He won't kiss her. He comes so close; his lips almost touch her. And then he pulls away.*

*"Do you want me to?" he asks, dropping his cigarette butt into the empty wine bottle.*

*"Yes, please."*

*He pushes her back onto the bed and works at her robe till she lies naked beneath him. His big hands move over her without touching.*

*"Please," she says again.*

*He sinks his teeth into the soft skin of her throat.*

*She understands the danger, but at least he's deigned to touch her.*

*Her hand finds his and he pulls away as if touched by a hot iron. Her blood is all he wants.*

She woke up. Jesus. She closed her eyes and tried to picture that same guy, whoever he was, kissing her this time, touching her face. But she couldn't manage it. Who was he? Who are these people in my dreams that I don't recognize? she wondered.

Beryl groaned and tumbled off the couch. She had spent the night in the living room, after walking home from Hermione's place.

Maybe Herm's geraniums were fine. Maybe she just imagined what she saw, put her own wilted thoughts onto the plants.

She threw on her uniform and left the house walking, as usual, before the sun was up. That was the thing she hated the most about her job—getting up so painfully early, too early even for the bus. Even in summer the sun wasn't up first for more than a few weeks. It couldn't be healthy.

Not that she'd have known if the sun was up on this day. It was solid grey without a dint in the clouds to remind you that things could be different.

She stopped for coffee at Robin's Donuts, where the only other customer was a dishevelled-looking man in blue clothes. A blue-collar worker stopping in on his way to the job. Just like her. Or maybe he was still on his way home from yesterday. Beryl felt afraid when she saw him out of the corner of her eye and sat as far away as possible at the other end of the shop.

The chair was cold and sticky against her thighs where her shorts ended. The morning was muggy but the coffee shop was icy cold. She faced the window and gazed out at the garbage and the empty sidewalk. The sky was pink in the east; the clouds had loosened up a little.

When the blue-clad man stood up to leave, Beryl turned and saw with a shock that it was Ed, her supervisor. He nodded at her as he walked by, but she couldn't manage a response till after he had passed.

"Good morning," she whispered, too late. He was gone.

How could I have not known that it was him? Beryl wondered, as she dug in her new bag for her glasses. This isn't good at all. I should have sat with him even if neither of us wanted me to.

She found her glasses in one of the compartments in her bag. She was still getting used to it with all its Velcro and buckles. It was too shallow; things fell out all the time. She'd lost her newspaper twice so far and once she hadn't found it again. It was just a matter of time before she lost someone's mail and then she would be in trouble.

Ed had asked Beryl to make a short report on her new bag: its pros and cons, her general thoughts on it. She happily did so, mostly singing its praises, but mentioning the shallowness of its pouches as a definite drawback.

She sighed and got up to leave, wondering how she could have been so blind. It wasn't that she hadn't seen him. She had seen him, and thought he was a sinister labourer on his way to another place, or on his way home from another day.

She didn't like the sense she'd had of him when she first walked into the coffee shop.

"It probably had more to do with me than him," she said out loud as she cut through an empty parking lot and continued on to the post office. So much spooky stuff has been going on lately.

She decided to try to remember to put her glasses on in the morning before there was any chance of running into anyone. Wearing glasses was still quite new for her and she didn't like it, didn't like the feel of the hardware on her face.

Maybe I'll treat myself this morning, she thought, stop at the cafeteria and grab myself a cinnamon bun. That was one thing that could be said for the post office: its cafeteria staff baked darn good sweet treats.

*Chapter 34*

Boyo fancies himself an exceptional follower of people; they never seem to notice him. Sometimes he feels invisible. Maybe I'll go to private detective school, he thinks, and hang out a shingle.

Following people gives him something to do that he really likes, a purpose. Imagine earning a living doing something so agreeable! It takes careful planning and he's so good at that sort of thing. Boyo flushes with pleasure.

He follows Beryl Kyte all the time—ever since she found the woman in St. Vital Park—and she doesn't have a clue. He's taken an interest in her, but wonders if she's simple. Like the cops. More likely, she's just oblivious to what's going on around her, like so many other people. Thinking girly thoughts, no doubt, about her hair and skin and weight.

Her skin and hair are distasteful: too white, too pale. She reminds him of something clammy that he can't quite grasp, doesn't want to grasp. She interests him, but he wouldn't want to touch her.

It's like with the hookers.

He used them to satisfy his needs. Sometimes he even fucked them. But he didn't touch them with his fingers if he could manage it.

He hasn't been to the Low Track for eighteen months. Nor has he used an escort service. For a long time he did one or the other at least six times a year.

Then three years ago he had a close call. They were in the back of his truck in a vacant lot off Higgins. The whore was new to him. She took the scarves in stride and said, "Whatever. I'm used to freaks."

He didn't liked that. He sat on her chest and felt her struggle, watched the terror in her eyes while he tightened the scarf around her neck.

"I should slice your head right off," he whispered between his clenched teeth.

When her eyelids closed he panicked. He scrambled into the front seat of the truck and tore through the streets to the emergency room at the Health Sciences Centre. He carried her inside the main doors and dumped her. It was a Saturday night and the place was a madhouse; no one in authority even saw him. He took off home and locked his truck in the garage where he left it for a very long time. It wasn't something he used often anyway.

The whore didn't die. At least, he supposed she didn't. It wasn't in the paper. And no one ever came looking for him. That was another good thing about whores. They were a tight-lipped bunch.

But it scared him enough that he didn't go back till eighteen months ago. When it all fell to pieces. Charise and her shaved cunt. Why'd she have to do it?

When Boyo sees Mail Girl Kyte pass through the employee entrance to the post office he eases himself off the little wall next to the library. Enough sitting around; he has places to be.

# Chapter 35

Beryl approached Ed's desk after stopping by the cafeteria for a bun. He was just sliding into his chair.

"Good morning," she said brightly.

"Hey, Beryl," Ed said, glancing up from the mess of paper on his desk. He looked, not at her, but at the gooey bun clutched in her fist.

But that was normal for Ed. He looked the same as he always did and again Beryl wondered if she'd imagined the sinister aspect of his presence at the coffee shop. She was probably projecting, or whatever they call it, when you force your own fears and thoughts onto someone else. Like she had done with Hermione's geraniums.

When Beryl got to her desk, Stan was sorting his mail, but there was something about the way he was doing it that gave her pause. He was usually a sorting machine, not even seeming to look at the letters as they flew from his hands into the case. This morning Stan was going slowly, examining each letter before he stuck it in its slot.

"You'll never get out of here at that rate, Stan," Beryl said, as she dragged his parcel bag over and deposited it at his feet. They took turns getting each other's bags.

Beryl began sorting; she glanced over at him. "Is everything okay?"

Stan looked at her, but didn't seem to hear. It was no wonder, with the conveyer belts roaring overhead. There was the screeching of a power saw this morning too, coming from the other side of the floor. And the constant high-pitched beep-beep of machinery backing up.

Beryl could taste the metal and the dust. Her hands were filthy, minutes after walking onto the sorting floor. She washed her hands so often they hurt. A layer of grimy dust seemed to coat her skin and clothing. The place was filthy; the bags that the mail went out in were filthy. And some of the workers were very strange.

Sorting mail, the indoor work, leaves plenty of space in the mind for all manner of thought: potent bubbles of imagination from countless sources mingled with the noise and the dirt.

The place seemed alive with danger to Beryl today. Anything could happen. Or more likely nothing. She didn't know which would be worse.

"Is something wrong, Stan?" she asked again.

This time he heard her and said, "Yes. We received some bad news at our house last night. Oh. Thanks for bringing my bag over."

Beryl stopped sorting and looked at him. Under the fluorescent lights his face was as white as a fish's underbelly.

"Did somebody die?" she asked and had the horrible feeling that there had been another killing and that Stan and his family were connected to it in some way.

Please don't let Stan be attached to a person who dies horribly, Beryl prayed. Please let all the deaths that he has to deal with be natural, happy deaths that take place at the right times.

"Yeah, somebody did die," Stan said. "Wally. Wally Goately."

"What?"

"Wally Goately died."

"Jesus. I just saw him last night," Beryl said. "He died?"

"Yes."

"What…what did he die from?"

"He choked to death on a chicken bone. He was eating alone at a restaurant and nobody noticed that he was choking until it was all over. His face turned blue."

Stan stopped sorting and looked at Beryl. "Where did you see him?"

"Oh God." Beryl sat down on her crooked little stool. "I saw him before he died, before he went into the restaurant, just outside of it. I was going to speak to him and then I didn't." My fault.

"I had to go and identify him," Stan said.

"Oh, Stan." Beryl stood up and moved to where he was leaning against his desk. She peered into his stunned face.

"You should go home."

"I can't. We don't get time off for distant cousins of wives," Stan said and went back to his new slow way of sorting.

"So what? You should go home anyway. You had to identify him and that must have been horrible. Does Ed know?"

"No."

Beryl turned abruptly and went to seek out her supervisor.

Ed said pretty much what Stan had said: You don't get days off for your own cousins, let alone for your wife's.

"Stan shouldn't have to be here, Ed. He had to identify the guy. He had to look at his face."

"Whose face?" Barry was glued to his computer, tapping keys.

"The guy's face!" Beryl slammed her hand down on his desk.

"So what are you, Stan's keeper?" Ed looked up from his work. "Can't he speak for himself?"

"You know what, Ed? Fuck off!" Beryl said, and knew that she had done absolutely nothing good for Stan or for herself.

"I'm so sorry, Stan," she said when she got back to her desk. She was shaking from having sworn at Ed. "How are Raylene and Ellie doing?" she asked. "They were both fond of Wally, weren't they?"

"Yeah, Ellie, especially. He was her new favourite uncle. God knows why! He was pretty good at playing with her, I guess."

"You should be home with them."

"It's okay. Raylene's sisters are there. I'd just be in the way. Besides, it's probably good if I get a chance to digest this awhile away from my family. I might be more good to them if I do."

Stan was probably right. Beryl regretted having spoken to Ed and she knew she had said too much; it wasn't her information to share.

Ed approached them then and gave Stan a soft punch on the shoulder. "You holdin' up okay, Sport?" he asked and Beryl could feel her face turn red.

Stan looked at her in stunned surprise and said, "Yeah, why wouldn't I be?"

"I heard you got some bad news last night," Ed said, also looking at Beryl.

"It's no big deal." Stan went back to his sorting.

Ed shuffled off and Stan called after him, "Ed!"

The supervisor turned around and Stan said, "Keep it under your hat, would ya?"

"Sure, Stan." Ed looked at Beryl again.

She was trying to sort but was blinded by tears. I'm a busybody, she thought. Just like Gladys Kravitz on *Bewitched*. Stan will hate me now and I can't bear it. Plus, I should have spoken to Wally last night. I should have sat with him while he ate and performed the Heimlich maneuvre when he started to choke. I could have done that.

"You shouldn't have told Ed," Stan said, barely sorting at all.

Tears streamed down Beryl's face as she stumbled over to his desk. She opened her mouth to apologize, but all she could do was gulp.

"Beryl, what is it?" Stan asked, alarmed. "You barely knew Wally. In fact, you didn't even like him. Did you?"

"I'm sorry, Stan. I'm sorry I told Ed. I thought he should let you go home." Beryl swallowed another gulp and then hiccupped. "But it wasn't my job to do that."

Stan put his arm around her shoulder. It was the first time he had ever touched her.

"Beryl, it's okay," he said. "It doesn't matter. Honest."

"I'm sorry, Stan," she said again. "I didn't mean to make anything worse."

"Seriously," Stan said, "it's not important."

Beryl blew her nose and tidied herself up some and Stan went back to his sorting.

"It's not so much that I have deep feelings for Wally," he said philosophically. "I don't. It's just that it's such a shock. So sudden, you know. One minute he's here, irritating as can be, and the next he's gone, all because of what he decided to have for supper."

*Chapter 36*

Beryl phoned Frank at work.

"I was wondering if you could tell me who discovered the body of Diane Caldwell," she asked.

"Pardon?" Frank sounded as though he were three thousand miles away.

"If you could tell me who found the woman in Whittier Park?"

Beryl knew that her deadheading experience, the pink collar on her cat, and now the changed furnace pegs had everything to do with her being the one who found the mushroom girl. She had no rational reason for believing this, but she knew it anyway.

Maybe whoever found the second dead person was having peculiar stuff happen at his home as well.

"Frank, could I talk to you in person, please? I think I may have something that will help."

Beryl wondered what her criminal would have done next if she'd had an old-fashioned thermostat.

Several years ago, when she'd had her furnace replaced, she had sprung for a new thermostat. It had a clock and little red and blue pegs to fasten in place at the times you wanted the furnace to warm up or cool down—red for warm, blue for cool. She could use them in the summer, too, for her air conditioner.

Beryl was fond of her thermostat pegs. During a heat wave, like the one that was suffocating southern Manitoba right now, she could set her air conditioner to come on half an hour or so before she figured she'd be home from work. Then, when she walked in the door, she would be greeted by a blast of cool air. Her cats would be huddled together on the couch for warmth.

Today, Beryl hadn't noticed that her yard was quiet when she entered it, that there was no hum from the air conditioner beneath her kitchen window.

Plus, her house was hot and she didn't notice that. She was thinking about Stan. And Wally. Would she have been able to save him if she had been there? Would she have had the confidence to perform the Heimlich on him? She could do it in her mind but she doubted if she'd be able to pull it off in real life. Maybe she could get someone to allow her to practise on him. Like Stan. Or Herm. Maybe Dhani. He'd probably let her. He'd probably even think it was a good idea.

She had just decided to give Dhani a call when she did notice something: Jude and Dusty had raced to the door to meet her. They ran around like kittens when they should have been snuggling on the couch trying to keep warm.

It was then that Beryl realized the air conditioner wasn't on. She checked the thermostat, turned it down and heard the click of the machinery as it began to work. So it wasn't broken, thank God. Next, she lifted up the flap to check that her blue and red pegs were in place. They were there all right, but they had been moved to times that made no sense. The blue peg was placed at three o'clock in the morning, for instance—the middle of nowhere, timewise. Someone had moved them. Someone had been in her house!

Now Beryl wished that the thermostat was just broken. At least then she could phone Winnipeg Supply and wait for them to come and banter with the repairman and talk about how jesusly hot it was.

She sat down at the kitchen table and cried. Tears of frustration and fear. He had been in her house, but it was like with the flowers and Jude's collar: she couldn't phone the police and tell them that the pegs on her thermostat had been moved. They would exchange glances amongst themselves and know that she had done it herself. Or worse, that she craved attention.

Had she done it herself? She didn't sleepwalk as far as she knew and surely that would be something that you'd know. No. This was not her doing.

Beryl looked around at her stuff. It looked as though nothing else had been disturbed, but she couldn't really be sure; her house was fairly messy. She checked the doors and windows and nothing looked wrong.

That was when she had decided It was time to confide in Frank.

He came right over. Beryl made iced tea and they sat outside on the deck, in spite of the heat and mosquitoes. She didn't want to be in the house. The guy had a key.

She told Frank everything—from her lobelia to her cat to her thermostat. She talked about the strange woman that Mrs. Frobisher had seen hanging around the house next door, and Clive's funny-smelling bed and the *Pilot Mound Sentinel.*

He didn't question her sanity or her memory or her intelligence. He believed her and she wished she had told him sooner.

Frank went to talk to Rachel Frobisher and Beryl phoned Noble Locksmiths to come and change her locks. She had decided too late to be careful with her key. But never again. She had vowed that it would never come to this, that she wouldn't buy into the fear that was advertised daily in the papers and on the tube. But now she found herself pondering an alarm system and bars on the windows.

"Dang," she said quietly and looked over her shoulder.

Frank came back and they went over to Clive's place to have a look around. This made Beryl nervous; she felt like a traitor. No one was home, as usual, and the door was locked for once. Frank considered breaking in and then decided not to.

Beryl remembered that she had a key; Clive had given it to her when she offered to phone someone about the vermin running rampant in his house. She hadn't done that yet.

She didn't offer the key to Frank, not after Clive's reaction to the idea of having police in his house. Frank didn't seem like a real cop to Beryl, but he was. That's why she had phoned him.

Guilt nudged her a little, but she decided if she was going to invade Clive's privacy she should at least warn him so he could tend to whatever contraband he was harbouring. In the meantime, she would go in after Frank left and gather up whatever she could find, in case he got serious about breaking in.

Beryl regretted involving Clive. It had been stupid and she felt her head heating up. She just hadn't been thinking. He'd never trust her again.

"Let me know when this Clive character comes back to town," Frank said, when they were back on the deck. "I think I should have a talk with him."

"Yes, all right," Beryl said.

"Do you know him very well?"

"Pretty well, I guess."

"The newspaper he gave you, do you still have it?"

"Yes!" Beryl leapt up. "I'm sure it's important. I'm just not sure how. When I went through it I couldn't find anything much except stories about 4-H Clubs and fiftieth wedding anniversaries and whatnot—ads for tractors and seed.

"Only one thing stood out for me, a sinister little obituary, but I can't for the life of me figure how it would connect to all this." She gestured around her.

"And I'm sure it has nothing to do with Clive," she added. "He didn't know what to make of it."

"May I see it?" Frank asked.

"And the pink collar?" he called after her when she headed inside to get it.

The collar was gone from its hiding spot in the north window well. Beryl shuffled the rocks around and wasn't surprised when she couldn't find it.

"It's gone," she said, handing the newspaper to Frank. "The collar's gone. I should have hidden it better. Like my house key."

"Yeah, it was pretty stupid of you to have a key outside like that. Anyone could have whisked it away and made a quick copy. Can I take this paper? I'd like to have a good solid browse through it."

"Sure." Beryl wished Frank hadn't said the word stupid in connection with her. Even if it was true.

"And I'll take the furnace pegs too. Maybe we can get something off them. Did you touch them?"

"No."

"I guess you and Clive have both touched the newspaper quite a lot."

"Yeah. I guess that was dumb too."

"Of course it wasn't. Neither of you would have been thinking in terms of fingerprints."

"No."

"Are you all right, Beryl?"

"I guess so. I just feel a little…unsafe. And stupid."

"Well, you're definitely not stupid. You are vulnerable. I'll stay with you till after the locksmith comes."

The air was still and heavy with moisture. The ice had melted in their glasses. Beryl was uncomfortable in her clothes.

"Frank?"

"Yes?"

"Would you mind if I went in and had a quick shower and got out of my postal outfit?"

"Go ahead. I'll be sitting right here." Frank looked sadly at his plastic chair. It was too small for him, looked as if it might stay attached to him when he stood up.

"Thanks… You can come in if you like—get away from the skeeters."

"That's okay. They don't bite me very often for some reason."

"Okay. I'll just be a few minutes."

Beryl didn't want to have to worry about having *Psycho*-type thoughts in the shower and at least for today she could avoid it. Unless, of course, Frank Foote was a policeman and a murderer as well, too evil even for mosquitoes to come near.

After her shower Beryl put on a pale yellow dress. Her feet were bare and she felt marvellously cool for a little while. When she joined Frank on the deck he was gazing off into the uppermost branches of the willow. She had expected to find him reading the *Pilot Mound Sentinal* and felt slightly let down. He sat with her till the locksmith arrived. And promised to stop in the next day, after she got home from work.

"I have a funeral tomorrow," Beryl said, "so I won't be here till a little later."

"Oh. I'm sorry."

"No. It's okay. It isn't someone I was close to. I'm going more out of closeness to his relatives." And because it's my fault he's dead.

"Well, I'll phone first." Frank stood up.

"This Clive that lives next door, is he the same Clive Boucher that used to play with Crimson Soul?"

"Yup, that's him," Beryl said. "And he still plays with them. That's why he's never home. He's always out on tour."

"I had no idea they were still together. I used to really like their music."

"It's not the same guys," Beryl said. "In fact, I think Clive is the only original band member. But they do play the old songs. They've got a young guy singer who's almost as good as Donny Swythins was. Still, it wouldn't be the same, would it?"

"No. I guess not," Frank said. "Remember that song…it went: 'Somebody said somebody saw you crying.' Something like that?"

Beryl smiled. "Yeah. It was laughing though. Somebody saw you laughing."

"Are you sure?"

"Yeah. And I'm afraid it wasn't Crimson Soul who sang it."

"You're kidding."

"No."

"Well, it's a great song anyway," Frank smiled.

"Yeah," said Beryl. "I love that song too. It's by a group called Man."

Frank hummed the line as he stepped down into the yard. At least that's what Beryl figured he must be doing. He couldn't carry a tune very well.

"I guess you've been fingerprinted," he said, "what with working for Canada Post. They did you, didn't they, when you first started there?"

"Yeah, they did," Beryl said. "Would my fingerprints have become part of some giant file, or will you have to go to the post office to get them?"

"No. They're part of a giant file."

"Good. I hate to think of you asking anyone at the post office for them. No matter how well you explained it, they'd think for sure I was a criminal. They wouldn't get it."

"We just need to discount them on the newspaper and the thermostat pegs."

"Yeah, I know that."

"Clive should come down too, so we can discount his as well."

"Does he have to?"

"Why? Will that be a problem for him?" Frank sounded very much like a policeman.

I mustn't forget that, Beryl thought, wanting to take the little newspaper back from Frank so she could roll it up and hit herself on the head with it. Nice as he is, this man is a cop. Clive doesn't need anyone searching his house or his past. For all she knew, his prints were already on file.

On the other hand this could be—probably was—a matter of life and death, especially death.

"No," Beryl said. "I'm sure it won't be a problem for him."

"Well, next time you see him, could you tell him to give me a call? It's possible this person may have left something else behind." Frank waved the *Pilot Mound Sentinel* in the air as he followed the crooked path into the back yard.

"Yeah, I'll tell him."

Beryl decided that after she went through Clive's house to hide his drugs and pipes and things that would connect him to hookers, and whatever the hell else, she would "remember" that she had a key and let Frank know. Or not.

"We won't be looking for anything else, Beryl," Frank said. "You can tell him that, too. If we find a little bit of pot or whatever, it doesn't matter. I'll make a point of being the guy who goes in, so that it won't get screwed up."

"Oh. I'm sure Clive leads a pretty clean life at this point, Frank. I mean he must be at least fifty-five."

"What's age got to do with it?" Frank chuckled.

Beryl liked his quiet chuckle. He stared off into space a lot, though, and she wasn't crazy about that. She was sweating now and it was only partially because of the heat. She wanted him to go. What kind of guy chooses to become a cop, anyway?

"Thanks, Frank. Thanks for everything. Especially understanding about how I think the stuff going on around here is connected to Beatrice Fontaine."

"That's okay, Beryl. Even if it isn't, someone has broken into your house for sure and probably Clive's."

Beryl remembered the question she had phoned Frank with in the first place.

"Who found Diane Caldwell?" she asked.

"Kids. Three young boys on their bikes—about eleven years old." Frank shook his head and looked at the ground. "Hell of a thing."

"I wonder if any creepy sorts of things have been going on at any of their houses," Beryl said. "That might be worth looking into."

"Yeah. That's a good idea. I'll call Katy Woodside in the Victims' Services Unit. She was going to be keeping an eye on the boys."

"They must be freaked," Beryl said.

"Yeah, I'm sure they are. Have you given any more thought to calling someone in the VSU?" Frank asked. "To talk?"

"No."

He slid behind the wheel of his vehicle. It was a different car today: a cop's car.

"Later in the week I have to go away for a couple of days," he said, "to a conference in Brandon. Just for part of two days—out on Thursday, back on Friday."

"Oh." Beryl didn't want Frank to go away, even if it was just for a short time. And even if he did gaze into the distance too much. He had something on his mind that had nothing to do with Beatrice Fontaine or Diane Caldwell. There was an underlying sadness about him. But that could probably be said of almost anyone. He just didn't hide his very well.

"I thought I should let you know in case you try to get hold of me," Frank said.

"Thanks."

"If anything comes up, you could phone Sergeant Christie. Do you have his number?"

"He gave it to me, but I threw it away," Beryl said. "I don't like him."

Frank wrote the number down on a piece of paper from his notebook.

"Did you steal a photograph off his bulletin board?" he asked.

"He told on me?"

"Yes."

"Steal is kind of harsh," Beryl said. "I think removed is more the word to describe what I did. It was a well-intentioned thievery at the very worst."

"Why did you do it?"

"Well…I don't know really. It just seemed wrong, her picture being on display like that. I guess I just wanted to sort of give her some privacy. Or something."

"Mm hmm…yes. I kind of figured it was something like that. I probably would've done the same thing if I'd seen it. Gregor shouldn't have had it up there in the first place." Frank turned the key in the ignition. "He's a jerk."

"Yeah, he is a jerk. I don't want to phone him," Beryl said, taking the slip of paper from Frank. "I will if I have to, but I hope nothing happens while you're out of town."

## Chapter 37

Beryl phoned Poulin's, described the problem at Clive's, and set up an appointment for later in the week. Then she went next door with the key to sniff out his drugs and paraphernalia. The place was still a sticky nightmare but she couldn't find anything that would incriminate him in any way. Clive must have gone through the place himself and taken care of things, in anticipation of a visit from the exterminators.

On the kitchen table, stuck to it actually, there was a business card for an outfit called "Long-stemmed Beauties," so Beryl put that in the pocket of her dress, unaware of the legalities of places with names like that. She locked the door behind her. Clive's place was ready for a visit from the cops. She hoped, if it came to that, Clive wouldn't hate her forever. Surely, if she explained everything, he would understand.

When Beryl stepped out into the late afternoon sunshine and heard the birds chirping and the squirrels chattering, the idea that these simple household oddities could be connected to two horrible deaths seemed so far-fetched that she wished she hadn't gotten Frank involved. But she knew that when she woke up cold in the middle of the night, she wouldn't feel that way.

Rachel was on a ladder washing her upstairs windows. They waved at each other. Beryl was reminded of all the house and yard work she had to do herself and she decided that this was a good time to get started.

She went inside the house and came right back out again. It was too dark in there. She got out her weeding cushion and started in on one of her flower beds, but the sight of the Chinese elms turned her stomach and she quit.

Beryl didn't know what to do. She wanted some breathing space, which she usually found at home. But these days her home didn't feel safe; it felt more like a place from which she needed to escape.

She thought about Dhani. She wanted to see him, yearned to see him, but she needed to sort out her thoughts first, to separate the different areas of her life into manageable sections that made sense.

Are the events of this summer going to ruin what we have? she wondered. Is our relationship going to be forever tainted by the gruesome actions of a psychopath?

Beryl went for a walk by the river. The river had been there her whole life and usually it was a comfort to her. But today all she saw were Chinese elms and purple loosestrife, the beautiful weed that was running rampant along this section of the Red River, choking the life out of the other vegetation.

## Chapter 38

At Wally's funeral Beryl sat near the back of the church and tried not to laugh. She recalled the Chuckles the Clown episode of the *Mary Tyler Moore Show*—the one where the clown was dressed up as a peanut and an elephant stepped on him and killed him. At least that's the way Beryl remembered it. Mary was disgusted with her co-workers for treating Chuckles' death in a light-hearted manner. And then, when it really mattered, during the solemn funeral service, the sensible Mary started to laugh and couldn't stop. Couldn't have stopped if the minister had shot her in the foot; if Lou Grant had keeled over and died right there, she couldn't have stopped laughing.

Wally's death was not funny. He had choked on a bone in a fried chicken joint and no one noticed in time to save him. No one noticed till he was on the floor, blue in the face, dead.

It definitely wasn't funny, especially not for Wally. Beryl swallowed her laughter and worried about hiccups. She tried to feel sad and couldn't. Just shaken. And guilty because of her growing dislike of Wally, which had kept her from approaching him on Sunday night. It wasn't her fault that he had died, but it still felt that way, just a little.

She was a bit awkward with Stan because she'd made no secret of her dislike for the dead man.

"Jesus, Stan," she could remember saying. "How could you be related to such an asshole? Are you sure he isn't dangerous?"

"Okay, firstly," Stan had said, "I'm not related to him. Raylene is. And she's pretty sure he was adopted so there's no actual blood tie at all. And secondly, shut up. He's not dangerous. He's just a pitifully neurotic loser who's really lonesome, so we're trying to include him in the odd thing. Raylene likes him and so does Ellie. In fact, my daughter is crazy about him.

"You didn't used to mind him so much, did you?" Stan went on. "You were nice enough to him at the folk festival."

"That was before I knew him very well. Like, I can't believe he came over to my house that day. And he thinks Hermione's weird."

"She is weird," Stan said.

"He called her a lesbian."

"She is a lesbian."

"Yeah, well, she is and she isn't. But Wally called her that as though it were a bad thing."

Stan had laughed and continued sorting his mail, faster than seemed humanly possible.

That was just a few days ago and now Beryl sat next to Stan at the funeral, feeling really bad.

"I'm so sorry, Stan," she'd said when she first sat down. And leaned over him to where Raylene sat quietly, red-eyed, her arm around their young daughter, Ellie. "I'm so very sorry, Raylene," she said. And to the kid, "I'm sorry about your Uncle Wally."

She hoped that Stan hadn't told his wife all the nasty things she had said.

Settling in beside him, Beryl looked straight ahead at the coffin which, thankfully, was closed.

"I'm really sorry," she whispered again, "for all the things I said. And did."

Stan smiled at her and patted her hand. "Not to worry."

She looked at him, her pale face pinched with anxiety.

"I mean it," he said, and squeezed her fingers. "Don't worry. It's okay."

Beryl was so relieved when he said that that she almost cried. She'd seen Raylene noticing Stan touching her and worried a little about that. She didn't want Raylene to think anything untoward was going on between her and Stan.

Now, as she struggled to squelch her laughter, she tried to get those tears back. She was so afraid she was going to laugh out loud. She thought of unpleasant things: the mushroom girl, Diane Caldwell, the ruined face of Hermione's customer, Jane. None of those worked, so she thought about the beach scene in *Saving Private Ryan*, the way she had felt what the soldiers must have felt when they pulled up in their boats. That knocked the laughs out of her.

She sat and worried about Stan. He seemed fine, but how could he not be disgusted with her? For how she behaved at work, the day after Wally's death, when she had been a blabbermouth and a terrible friend?

Ed had already given her a notice requesting her presence at a counselling session for what he had labelled "insubordination." She accepted it from him meekly, without question, and he seemed surprised by that.

"It's for telling me to fuck off," he said.

"Yeah, I figured that," she had replied and stuck the notice in her mail-bag.

Beryl's gaze wandered over the sparse gathering of people who had come to say good-bye to Wally Goatley. Stan and Raylene were the only ones she knew.

Once the service began, she found herself staring at the back of one man's head. It was so familiar. He turned to catch her staring, as though he felt her eyes on him. An icy spider crawled its way up the length of Beryl's spine. It was Joe Paine. He gave her a slight nod and turned back to the words of the minister.

"What the hell is he doing here?" she whispered to Stan.

"Shh!" said Stan who was listening attentively to the minister's ideas on a very odd man he had never met.

Beryl came to understand something new on the day of Wally's funeral. She learned it from a seven-year-old girl. And Raylene. It was about the wherefores and the whys of angels and heaven and what you do for yourself and others when people you love up and die on you.

It was an automatic thing, but one with which Beryl had no experience. She realized it must have been all around her, but she had never seen it or even thought about it till Wally died.

People invented things: beautiful truths of their own that suited them and that they hoped would soothe the ache inside the child who asked the inevitable questions.

"Why did Uncle Wally have to die?"

"God took him, honey, because he needed another angel in heaven."

"Is Uncle Wally an angel?"

"He sure is, Ellie. God looked all over Winnipeg till he found Uncle Wally and then he said, 'He's the one I need.'"

"When I die, will I be an angel?"

"Yes, you will."

"Will I be able to be an angel with Uncle Wally? Will I see him in heaven when I die?"

"Yes, you will."

"For sure?"

"Yup, for sure. You and Uncle Wally will be side by side in heaven."

Then later, "Why did God have to pick Uncle Wally?"

And it would begin again: a variation on a theme. One that was old, but brand new; one that tried to ease the pain on a shiny little face that had never known suffering like this before; one that was almost, but not quite, acceptable.

There was a part two to this thing that Beryl learned. She saw suffering on the mother's face as she tried to protect her daughter. Ellie's misery was Raylene's own. Beryl envied her that misery.

The reception that followed the funeral took place in another room in the church, where fancy sandwiches and dainties were piled on plates, and bustling church ladies tended giant urns of coffee and tea. They had never heard of Wally Goately. But Raylene was a church goer and Ellie went to Sunday school here.

"Did you know that Joe Paine knew Wally?" Beryl asked Stan when they stood alone at the table of dainties.

"What?"

"Didn't you see him upstairs at the service?"

"No."

"Well, he was there. That's what I was trying to tell you when you told me to shut up."

"I didn't tell you to shut up."

"Well, as good as."

"Anyway, are you sure?" Stan asked. "I didn't see him. I didn't know he knew Wally. Are you sure it was him?"

"Yeah, I'm sure. He even nodded at me."

Raylene motioned to Stan from across the room and he moved off to join her and Ellie.

Beryl wondered if the sight of Joe Paine upstairs had been a hallucination. She wondered, not for the first time lately, if maybe she was going insane.

Fancy sandwiches were one of her favourite things but she couldn't enjoy them under the circumstances. She kept thinking Joe was going to creep up behind her, or an imaginary Joe, so she found a chair against a wall and sat.

There was no reason for her to be here any longer. It was time to go, but a huge tiredness held her in the chair. It seemed as if death was all around her. She had gone through life with someone dying every few years, like most people, she supposed. But now it seemed there was no reprieve. Every time she woke up someone else was dead. Every time she turned around there was a girl with mushrooms growing out of her mouth or a man with a chicken bone lodged in his throat.

## Chapter 39

It was dusk by the time Beryl left Stan and Raylene's house on Eugenie Street. Not wanting to be alone, she had followed them to their place and stayed too long, colouring with Ellie in her Cinderella colouring book.

She walked by Hermione's shop on the way home and saw that the shades were down and the lights were out. It was dark upstairs too, where Hermione lived, but Beryl thought she heard a man's laughter coming from the open window. She crossed the street, cut through the park and walked on to her own house where she locked herself inside.

There was a message from Frank. "Just checking in. Phone, if you like." A reminder that he'd be going to a conference in Brandon for the better part of two days.

Beryl opened her bedroom window, the one that faced Lyndale Drive and the river, straining to hear more laughter from somewhere, straining to hear anything at all. But it was quiet now, except for the odd car swishing through the puddles left from today's rain. The damp soft air felt cool against her hot face. There was warm in it too, in the middle of it for a second. She lay on her bed, trying to think of something good, something in her life that felt as hopeful as that trace of warm air running through the cool.

Dhani came to mind and she tried to hang on to him as she drifted off, willing her dreams to be of him.

But instead she dreamed that she was having a party.

*When the day arrives, no one can get in. They try to come, they arrive carrying bottles of wine and trays of fancy sandwiches and wearing smiles from ear to ear. But they can't get up her steps and in her door. They slip and slide and fall right down. Some people hurt themselves. And Beryl can't get out to them. She has an idea that if she can just make it out to the deck, they can have the party out there. If anyone has to go to the bathroom, they can use the bushes; she has lots of bushes. But she can't get out. Her guests mill around outside for a bit, and every now and then someone has another go at getting in, but before long they up and leave. And they are no longer happy. Beryl calls to them from a window but they can't hear her; they can't see her either.*

Beryl woke up lonesome and depressed and wished she could stop thinking and dreaming about having a party. No one would come. And if they did come, what if they couldn't get in? What if she couldn't get out? What if people fell and hurt themselves and sued her?

Hermione's light was on upstairs and there was no man's laughter coming from the open window. Beryl took a chance and, passing the pots of sickly looking geraniums, climbed the outside steps to her friend's apartment. Worry scrunched up Hermione's wide forehead, making wiggly vertical lines between her nicely shaped eyebrows.

"What is it, Beryl...sweetheart...what?"

Beryl began to cry and Hermione hugged her close and led her over to the couch. She poured brandy into a tea cup and held it out to Beryl. The fire of the brandy licked through her. Her friend's comfort brought more tears and a feeling so strong Beryl wasn't sure she had ever felt it before.

Hermione moved the hair out of Beryl's eyes and hugged her for a long time. I love you, Beryl thought, but she didn't say it. She didn't want to scare this precious gift out of her life and maybe words of love would do that.

This was the second time lately that she had to force herself not to say *I love you* and she supposed that was a good thing. Words of love straining to escape.

"What's the matter with your geraniums?" she said instead.

Hermione sighed and took a short swig of the brandy straight from the bottle.

"I don't know. I have an appointment with someone at the university tomorrow. I'm taking in some plants and the dirt surrounding them to see if they can help me get to the bottom of it. I have a feeling somebody poisoned them or something."

"Jesus."

"Yeah. It's terrifying, really."

"Do you feel safe here?" Beryl asked.

"No."

"Would you like to come and stay at my house?"

"Do you feel safe at your house?"

"No."

Hermione smiled.

"At least there would be the two of us," Beryl said.

Hermione drank again from the bottle. "You're welcome to stay here, if you like."

"Thanks, Herm, but I think I'll get on home. I have to be at work in a few hours." She sighed. "God, I'm so tired."

Beryl walked home, avoiding the park, sticking to the well-lit streets, wishing she were in bed asleep already. She wondered if wishing she were asleep all the time was the same as wishing she were dead.

*Chapter 40*

Two days later Stan marched right up to Beryl when he got to work, before even pouring himself a cup of coffee. She watched him approach, thinking how much he looked like Cliff Claven with his blockhead pants and brush mustache.

"Rollo isn't dead!" he announced.

"Who?" she asked. She was sitting at her desk, drinking her first coffee of the day.

"Dr. Paine's cat, Rollo. He's not dead. I saw him yesterday, lying on a couch in the waiting room. At first I thought it must be a new cat, one that looked a lot like Rollo, but I looked close. I've had dealings with Rollo; I know him. It was him all right."

Beryl squeezed her eyes shut against the overhead drone. And something solid was being cracked open somewhere, not too far away. The head-splitting racket of a jackhammer hurt more than just her ears.

"Stan. What are you saying?" She opened her eyes for a second and closed them again to shut out the glare of the fluorescent lights.

"I'm saying that Joe Paine's cat is alive and well. You were right not to trust that lying brain-sick fuck bucket."

"Did you see Joe? Did you ask him about it?"

"No. I had just stopped in to make an appointment for Scrug. I didn't think I should say anything to anyone before checking with you."

"Good."

"It feels very…well, strange," Stan said. "I wonder what he would have said if I had seen him and offered my condolences. I guess he would just have denied ever having said such a thing. I mean, Rollo was right there! Dr. Paine was lying!

"And you say you saw him at Wally's funeral?" he went on. "What the hell's that all about?"

"I don't know. I don't know. Sit down!" Beryl was trying to think what all of this could mean, but she couldn't get anywhere with it. All she could see right now was that for some crazed reason Joe had lied about Rollo's death. The most likely reason seemed to be so that he could elicit her sympathy, but what a strange time to have done it, when they had just discovered a dead woman in the woods.

Or, maybe he knew he was going to start to cry and that embarrassed him and he felt he should have a good excuse for it, so made up the first thing that came to mind. As if the mushroom girl wasn't enough!

Or, maybe he was a murderous lunatic and this was just the tip of the iceberg.

"I'm not sure what to do about this," Beryl said.

"Yeah, I know what you mean," Stan replied. "It's not exactly the kind of thing you report to the police."

"I think I can, though," Beryl said. "I think I should tell Frank. He was really good at taking the lobelia and furnace pegs and things seriously. This is kind of like that, isn't it?"

"Well…I don't know. Maybe. Yeah, I guess," Stan said. "God, this is so bizarre. I wonder if Dr. Paine is crazy. Why would anyone who loves his pet as much as he loves Rollo, or says he does, lie and say that he was dead? God, I just can't believe he's evil, Beryl. Scrug loves him so much."

"When did you make the appointment for?" Beryl asked.

"This afternoon."

Ed sauntered over to them at this point and said, "Any chance of either of you two working extra hours today? We're really short of bodies this morning."

"No, thanks," they said in unison.

"It would really be appreciated. We're gonna have to order some people back today if I don't get more volunteers," Ed said.

"No," said Stan.

"You can't force people," said Beryl.

"We'll pay you for three hours if you do just one or two hours of extra work," Ed wheedled.

"Yeah, right," Stan said. "It never turns out to be nearly as much fun as you say it's gonna be, Ed. Why don't you suggest to some of those neckties upstairs that they hire some full-time employees to do this job?"

"It's not up to me. You know that."

"The overtime is killing us as it is. I'm gonna be working extra hours on my own route today, for Christ's sake. Do you want me to die on the job? Is that what you want?"

"No, Stan. I don't want you to die."

Ed was backing up now, moving off in the direction of his desk.

"We're saying no!" Stan shouted after him and a few of the others in the aisle started in with a little chant, "Saying no! Saying no! Saying no!"

Beryl and Stan smiled at each other.

"I'm going to phone Frank," Beryl said.

She followed Ed, who had a phone in his pocket. Then she turned around and came back.

"I can't phone him," she said. "He's in Brandon till tomorrow on some course or retreat or something."

"Can't you call him on his cell phone?" Stan asked.

"I don't even know if he has one."

"He must have one. He's a policeman," Stan said. He was sorting mail at the speed of light. "What should we do?"

"I don't know. Let's think it over during our walks and then discuss it after work before you take Scrug in for…what are you taking him in for?"

"He's having a little trouble going number two."

"Oh. Poor old Scrug; that can't be fun."

"No. I just hope it's nothing serious, like a massive growth or something."

Stan's sorting went back to the way it was the day after Wally's death. Slow and studied.

"Don't worry, Stan. He's probably okay. He's just getting kind of old."

"I don't want him to get old."

Exhaust fumes were coming up from the basement where the trucks parked. They mixed with the usual stench of oil and dust and Beryl felt as though she was suffocating. She stepped up her sorting. The sooner she was done, the sooner she would get a breath of fresh air.

# Chapter 41

The phone rang late that afternoon and Beryl let the machine pick it up. She never did otherwise anymore. It was Stan, so she answered.

"Beryl, I'm coming over," he said.

"What's up? Are you home already?"

"Yeah."

"How's Scrug?"

"He's okay. Dr. Paine just gave me a laxative for him. We'll see how that goes."

"Okay, so what happened?"

"I'm comin' over," Stan said.

"What happened?"

"I want to talk in person."

Beryl's temples began to throb. She turned the heat off under her tomato soup and went out to the deck to lie down on her lounger.

She had found a can of mushroom soup in her pantry and had begun spooning it into the pot before she gagged, her body remembering her feelings about mushrooms, even if her head didn't. She threw the soup away and dug around for a can of tomato.

Now Beryl and the mosquitoes waited for Stan.

They had decided that he would mention Beryl to Joe in passing, not in connection with the mushroom girl, just in an I-think-we-have-a-friend-in-common kind of way, and see what he said, just to tread around him a little on a subject that wasn't connected to animals.

Beryl trusted Stan to be gentle in his probing and not to do any blurting, like: Why the hell are you going around saying Rollo is dead? What's the big idea?

They didn't want to wreck anything while they waited for Frank to come home. They didn't want Joe Paine running away.

Stan cut through the house to get to the deck, stopping at the fridge for a beer.

"You should lock your back door if you're gonna be sitting out here," he said.

"I knew you'd be here in a minute."

"Still…"

"Yeah, I know. Okay. What happened?"

"I'm warning you. It's weird."

"What, Stan?"

"He says he's never heard of you."

"What?"

"Joe Paine has never heard of you and I think he's telling the truth."

"How could that be?"

Stan sat down in one of the green plastic chairs and took a long pull on his Fort Garry Pale Ale. He was still in his post office clothes.

"Is it possible," he asked, "that the guy who you met is a different Joe Paine? One that isn't a vet?"

"I didn't make up the part about him being a vet," Beryl said. "I had never heard of him before, remember? It was you that was all excited about him. He told me he was a vet. I remember it clearly. He said: I'm a veterinarian. I remember thinking that it was an odd thing for him to say at such a time, with a woman lying dead just a few yards away. Like, who cared what his occupation was? It wouldn't have occurred to me to say: I'm a letter carrier."

Beryl stopped talking and Stan stopped drinking and they stared at each other for a long moment.

"Let's take me to your Dr. Joe Paine and show him to me," Beryl said.

"Yes. Let's."

They hopped into Stan's junk heap of a car—a 1976 Buick. Actually, the car belonged to his older daughter, the one whose ass he thought the sun shone out of. She had lent it to him while she traipsed around the British Isles.

In less than five minutes they were at the Becker Animal Hospital.

Beryl hung back a little as they approached the front door. She wasn't totally confident that the person she was about to encounter wouldn't be the strange and troubled man that had cried the first time he met her. And she did not want to see that man.

Stan went in first and she followed. There were two women in the reception area, busy on phones, and one man in a white smock studying a chart. And there was a Siamese cat, making quite a ruckus in its cage while its master tried to soothe it with little clucking sounds. Rollo was the cause of the disturbance; at least Beryl assumed it was Rollo, since he seemed to have the run of the place. He sat a few feet away from the cage staring calmly at the cat.

The man in the smock looked up and smiled when they came in. He wasn't fat but he had a substantive air about him, as though he enjoyed eating and cooking and trying new recipes. Not unlike Frank Foote in his physical presence, but with a twinkle in his eye instead the sadness. And he looked to be about Frank's age, fifty or so.

"Hello again, Stan. Did you forget something?" he asked.

"Hi, Dr. Paine," Stan said. "Yeah, I forgot to pick up dog food while I was here."

"How did you get along administering the laxative to Scrug, or have you tried it yet?"

"Yeah, I did it as soon as I got home and he seemed to actually like it."

Dr. Paine laughed. "Yeah, a lot of dogs do. It's our most popular laxative. Be sure to keep in touch. Let me know if things don't get any better and we'll figure out what to do next."

"Thanks, I will."

Stan bought a bag of dry dog food that he didn't need and they went back outside.

"It's not him," Beryl said and sat down on the front steps of the animal hospital. "Stan. It's not him."

He sat down beside her.

"I'm sorry for not introducing you. I didn't think we should confuse the issue any more before we talk to this Frank of yours. It was enough that I tried to insist that he knew a Beryl Kyte earlier in the day without actually introducing him to one later."

"This is majorly mind-boggling," Beryl said.

"It seems unbelievable to me that the police don't know about this," Stan said. "I mean, they would have had to talk to the guy pretending to be Joe Paine again after that day, wouldn't they?"

"I don't know. They never tried to talk to me again after that day," Beryl said, "at least not after the day I went in to give my statement. Except for that jerk, Christie, calling to see if I stole his photo. And that wouldn't have happened if I hadn't taken it. Probably the guy who said he was Joe didn't steal anything from the police station. "Let me just think about something for a minute," Beryl said.

They sat quietly on the step while she tried to order her thoughts about the morning in St. Vital Park.

"He told me his name was Joe Paine," she said finally. "That doesn't necessarily mean he told the cops his name was Joe Paine. I don't know what he said to them. He said it, whatever it was, a ways away from me. I remember watching him talk to them, but at a distance; I didn't hear him. He could have told them his name was Joe Christ for all I know.

"And," she went on, "when he made the call on his phone, I think he said: my name is Joe. I don't think he gave a last name at all. God, I wish Frank was here."

"We've got to phone the police anyway," Stan said. "Frank or no Frank, we can't not phone them with this information."

"Are you thinking that this other Joe, whoever he is, is the killer of the two women?" Beryl asked.

"Well, yeah. Aren't you?"

"Yeah. I guess I am. His behaviour has just been too…out there. It really creeps me out to think I was alone with him and I've talked to him on the phone and everything."

"I think you're in danger, Beryl. And Hermione's probably in danger too."

"Well, if he doesn't know that we know he's not Joe Paine, then nothing's that different."

"What if he does know? What if he's been spying on us today? He could be watching us right now for all we know." Stan looked nervously over both shoulders.

"He attacked both women in the parks where they were jogging. He didn't abduct them or anything. That's not the way he operates."

"Beryl, he's wacko. We don't know how he operates. We don't know how his demented mind works. Do you think he sticks to a schedule with no room for alternatives? He's hardwired differently from me and you. He could do anything!"

"God. Maybe he was planning on killing me that day in the park."

"Maybe."

"I wonder why he didn't?"

"Maybe you're not tall enough, or skinny enough. I don't know."

"He told me he walked there every Saturday morning and I believed him," Beryl said. "Let's go back to my house. I'm going to phone my good friend, Sergeant Christie."

"Good."

Sergeant Christie wouldn't give Beryl the information she wanted: the other Joe's last name. He didn't even think about it, just said no, right off the bat. She wished now she'd been nicer to him and that she hadn't been stupid enough to steal the picture off his bulletin board. She didn't know who else to ask for, or what else to tell him, so she hung up.

This didn't sit well with Stan. He thought they should be telling somebody everything they knew.

Beryl was of a mind that things could get messy and unpleasant if they didn't wait for Frank. Maybe it was too much television or maybe just the general paranoia she had been feeling lately. She just didn't trust Gregor Christie and his unpleasant attitude.

She pressed redial and got the sergeant again.

"Could you please tell me when Inspector Foote will be back?" she asked.

"Tomorrow," he said.

"Um…about when tomorrow, do you know?"

"No."

She hung up and turned to Stan. "I'm waiting for Frank," she said. "He'll be back tomorrow."

"In that case, both you and Hermione are sleeping at our house tonight," Stan said. "No arguments."

"You won't get one from me," Beryl said. "Let's stop at Herm's without warning and kidnap her."

"I'll phone Raylene and tell her what she's in for."

"Just a sec."

Beryl dialled the main switchboard at the police station and asked for Frank Foote's cell phone number. To her surprise, they gave it to her.

She dialled it and a girl answered.

"Is Frank Foote there, please?"

"He's out of town for a couple of days. May I take a message?"

"Uh…is this his cell phone?"

"Yes."

"Uh…"

"I'm his daughter, Sadie. Can I help you?"

"Oh. Uh…I guess he doesn't have his phone with him then, in Brandon."

"No. He left it with my sister, Emma, so she can keep track of my brother and me while he's away."

"I see. Okay…"

"Emma's doing the laundry."

"Oh. And your dad will be back tomorrow, will he?"

"Yes. In the afternoon sometime."

"Okay. Thanks, then, Sadie. If he phones home could you please tell him that Beryl Kyte is hoping very much to talk to him?"

"Sure."

At least Sadie had been more forthcoming than Sergeant Christie. Beryl wondered if she should have tried to get a number for Frank in Brandon. But she kept thinking maybe she was overreacting or confused, that there would be simple explanations for everything and she would end up feeling like an idiot.

She left Stan to phone Raylene and threw a few things into her backpack.

"How did this guy know that I didn't know Dr. Paine, that I wouldn't know right off that he was impersonating him?" Beryl asked when Stan hung up the phone. "Dr. Paine could very easily be Jude and Dusty's vet."

"Probably he took a chance and lucked out," Stan said.

"But what an odd chance to take. What an odd thing to do."

"Yeah."

"Let's pick up snacks and booze and stuff on the way," Beryl said, her voice a little higher-pitched than usual. "Let's not go to work tomorrow."

"It's not a party, Beryl. You're hiding out at my house."

"That doesn't mean we can't have fun. Should I bring my Trivial Pursuit game? Or Scrabble?"

"Yeah, okay. Just Trivial Pursuit, though, not Scrabble," Stan said. "I don't like Scrabble; I never win.

"I'm a little worried about all the tall thin customers of Hermione's that aren't coming to my house tonight," he went on.

"Well, at least the police were sensible enough to make that stuff public information," Beryl said. "And they contacted all Herm's clients, tall and thin, short and thin, tall and fat—all of them—to warn them that they are especially vulnerable."

"Yeah, that's good."

Beryl explained the plan to Dusty and Jude while giving them a gentle pat. Then she turned the key in her new lock and followed Stan out to the old Buick.

## Chapter 42

The next day was Friday. Beryl phoned Frank at work as soon as she woke up, just in case. He wasn't there, but they assured her he'd be back behind his desk sometime in the afternoon. Then she phoned her own home for messages but there was nothing new.

It was strange waking up at Stan's. She'd slept on a pull-out couch in the basement. She would have been sharing it with Hermione but they hadn't been able to find her.

When they went by her shop they found the blinds pulled down and a note on the door in her backhanded scrawl: Closed for a few days.

Beryl ran up the stairs to the flat and knocked on the door, knowing she wouldn't get an answer. The blinds were pulled in the upstairs apartment as well.

"Well, this is probably a good thing," Stan said. "She's gone somewhere safe."

"It feels so empty, though," Beryl said, "like no one lives here anymore."

"It's only temporary," Stan said, when they were back outside. "A few days." He pointed to the wrinkled note.

"I wish she had phoned me," Beryl said.

"Maybe she will yet."

"I could phone home for messages from your house."

"Yeah. Come on, let's go. This place is too quiet."

"Stan?"

"Yes?"

"Look at the geraniums."

Those that weren't completely dead had wilted, sickly looking leaves. There were no live blooms.

"Stan, these flowers used to be the healthiest, happiest, most exuberant flowers in Winnipeg."

"Let's get out of here," Stan said, and they drove to his place, where Beryl holed up with the Socz family for the night.

When she had phoned home for messages yesterday there had been two hang-ups, a message from the library saying she had a book waiting, and one from Dhani. He wanted to set something up for the weekend.

Beryl had returned his call when she was able to get some privacy after Ellie went to bed. She brought him up to speed as best she could. Dhani wanted to know everything, but she held back a little. It was difficult on the phone to talk about the complicated parts. She assured him that she was safe and that she would call him again when there was something more to tell. And she promised to introduce him to Stan and Raylene soon.

Now it was morning and Beryl was rethinking her plan of taking the day off. Her work ethic won out. She liked to think she was the type of person who could wake up feeling okay and phone in sick, but she wasn't. And she didn't feel like going home. Dusty and Jude would be fine. She had left lots of food and water out for them and they had each other for company.

Plus, it was the day she was to be officially hollered at. She didn't think she should miss that; it would be too noticeable.

It had been years since she'd been yelled at in an official capacity. Last time, it was for storming out and not coming back one day, when the noise had seemed so loud she thought her head would explode. When she had complained, they sent some joker with an official noise measuring device who found that the noise was at an "acceptable level" unless it kept up for prolonged periods of time.

"Doesn't all the fucking time count as prolonged?" she had shouted.

The official had looked uneasy and had been assured by her supervisor at the time that the noise was only intermittent. Beryl had had a different supervisor then, a woman, who was no help at all.

Stan lent her a post office shirt now, too big, of course, but it didn't matter. The shirt was clean and even ironed; Raylene ironed Stan's shirts for him. Beryl wore her own shorts, the ones she had been wearing the night before. If they wanted to yell at her for that, they could do it at the same time as her insubordination counselling. Kill two birds with one stone.

"Do you have a union steward going in with you?" Stan asked. "In case they start saying things they aren't supposed to. That happens sometimes, ya know. And you probably wouldn't notice."

"Yes, I would." Beryl twirled around in front of the full-length mirror in Stan and Raylene's front hallway. She liked the look of Stan's shirt on her. It was huge.

"I've got Bert Wheeler going in with me," she said. "He's pretty good, isn't he?"

"Yup, he knows his stuff," Stan said. "That's good."

Beryl made short work of her route. It was one of those great mail days that come a few times each summer, when there are no bills and no cheques, no *Chatelaine* magazines or *Reader's Digest*s, and most importantly, no flyers. Just a bit of this and a bit of that. It was like a gift. Beryl sailed through the streets with her mind on what was to come.

As the morning went by she felt less and less like being hollered at. The counselling session wasn't till the afternoon. What a waste of a great mail day! Maybe I'll miss it, she thought.

She rummaged through her bag for the notice that Ed had given her. It was gone. It must have fallen out of her too-shallow mailbag. She decided to use the shallow bag as an excuse for not showing up. Her problems with the bag were well documented:

she had filled out a form. Plus she'd done a fair bit of whining about it out loud; that should help.

The only problem was Bert Wheeler. She didn't want to let her union steward down. He was such a nice guy.

Then she figured, what the heck.

As soon as she was finished her walk, Beryl went to the third floor of the Centennial Library to look up Hortense Frouten's obituary in the *Winnipeg Free Press*. Word for word, it was the same as the one in the *Pilot Mound Sentinel*, except for two small additions.

First, there was an extra name: Keller. Hortense Frouten Keller, it read. Beryl supposed she must have married after she had left Pilot Mound for the city. Whoever wrote the obituary didn't think her married name would be of interest to the folks back home.

The second addition was the fact that she had been buried in Brookside Cemetery. That's actually what it said: Hortense Frouten Keller has been buried in Brookside Cemetery. Beryl had never seen such an obituary. Didn't they usually use words like interment and final resting place and whatnot?

She stopped at the counter on the first floor and picked up the book that was waiting for her: Larry McMurtry's latest, the only one of his she hadn't read.

Beryl used a pay phone in the library. Frank still wasn't back. She decided to take a trip to Brookside Cemetery and look for the grave of this Hortense Frouten Keller. She waited in the hazy heat of midday for a bus that would take her to Red River College. From there it was just a short walk to the graveyard.

She had heard Ariadne Kruck-Boulbria bragging one day to her neighbour to the south about how she and her husband would often go for brisk walks in the cemetery during their lunch hours to get some fresh air and exercise. She had used some stupid word when she was talking about it, something like "couched." As in: Yes, here we are getting all this fresh air and exercise couched in a stroll through Brookside Cemetery.

Beryl could just picture them, her, anyway, moving her arms in an exaggerated manner, driving Mort bonkers with her healthy ideas.

She got off the bus at the college and made the short trek to the graveyard. It was a beautiful spot, huge, with grand old oaks and maples. And a brook running through it.

The August sun was so bright it hurt. Beryl was glad she had worn her sunglasses.

A number of Canada geese were paddling in the water and poking around among the gravestones, on their way south already. Surely they were jumping the gun. It was so warm yet, but anything could happen, Beryl knew, now that it was August. She supposed they knew what they were doing.

Unlike her. Here she was in a cemetery on the edge of town, wandering around looking for the grave of a woman she had never met, who could very easily not be connected to anything that mattered to Beryl.

But it felt important; it felt like the key. She tried to be methodical in her search. There was a lot of territory to cover. But every now and then she would get caught up and head off on a tangent—if she found some especially old graves, say, from the 1800s or graves with familiar names carved into the granite. Then she would haul herself back and try to inject some new order into her plan and hope that she hadn't missed anything.

Some of the headstones were unreadable, the engraving worn away by decades of Winnipeg winters, or hidden under moss or mould that had grown right into the lettering. But those were the very old ones.

It took almost two hours of searching. In fact, she had almost given up. She had begun to wonder if the writer of the obituary had just buried the woman here himself and not bothered with a marker of any kind. She knew she would be looking for something small at best—certainly not ornate—probably the kind that lay right on the ground.

And then she found it in the middle of a young dogwood, barely visible inside the lush growth: Hortense Frouten Keller, Born 1933—Died 1981.

Beryl gently moved the young branches aside. No "Rest in Peace"; no "Beloved Mother, Daughter, Sister, or Aunt"; nothing of that nature. Nothing more at all.

She thought she heard train cars banging together in a rail yard nearby. A loud sound, but one she didn't disapprove of. She'd lived near the tracks all her life.

Beryl was afraid. She had no parents, no siblings, a few cousins she had lost track of, and a few friends. Her own gravestone could well be as bleak as this one. She decided to write down her arrangements when she got home, cremation for sure and a scattering to the four winds—so no future gravestone readers would pity her the way she pitied Hortense Frouten Keller. God, even her name was dreadful.

The noise turned out to be thunder. Lightning flashed in the darkened sky. It was just three o'clock in the afternoon, but it was darker than dusk. Beryl hadn't noticed the change in the light and realized she still wore her sunglasses. She took them off now to have a better look at the grave.

It wasn't well-tended but neither had it been ignored. There were offerings of a sort, and it was only when she crouched to look more closely through the shrubbery that the blood ran cold in her veins.

The rain started up but she didn't notice. She knelt down on the wet grass and forced herself to examine what lay before her. This time she had the sense not to touch, except for the branches. She had to touch those.

The dead geraniums were the first things that caught her eye. Faded now, but formerly the bright scarlet variety, one of the types that Hermione favoured.

And a scarf. The kind that Beryl's grandmother had worn, to "spruce up an outfit," as she used to say. It looked to be made from nylon. And it had been a long time since this scarf had spruced up any outfits. Suddenly Beryl knew that this was the weapon used to strangle Beatrice Fontaine. She remembered the way Frank had described the scarf tied around Diane Caldwell's throat, described it to Hermione, that is. An old-lady scarf was what he had called it. Well, that's what this was.

There were two more items. One was a digger with a triangular point, like the one Frank had talked about, that had been used to gouge out Diane's eyes.

And the other item was a jar. Beryl didn't want to look closely because she already knew what was in it: the eyes of Diane Caldwell. But she did look, just for a second. And then she screamed, not knowing, when she stopped, if it had been out loud. Maybe it was just inside her head.

She could see a couple running toward her through the rain and realized then that her scream had not been silent. The look of alarm on both their faces told her this.

It was the Kruck-Boulbrias.

Beryl closed her eyes and began to shake.

Ariadne was suddenly on her knees with both arms around Beryl. Ariadne didn't feel bony at all, not like Beryl figured she would, not like most of the other people she knew. She felt rounded and soft and supple and wet and she hugged Beryl close and pushed her hair out of her eyes.

"Beryl, what is it?" she asked.

Mort stood in the background with a look of concern on his face.

Why had she been so quick to judge these people? They were her saviours.

"It's so complicated I don't know if I can even begin," Beryl said in a faltering voice. "But I have to go to the police. I have to go to a particular policeman."

"Frank Foote?" Mort asked, with his phone already in his hand.

"You know him?" Beryl asked, and then remembered the ball game in Whittier Park, the two familiar men in their uniforms.

"Yes. Frank and I play on the same softball team," Mort said. "I saw you two waving at each other a while back."

He moved underneath the branches of a giant blue spruce where the rain didn't penetrate and went through a series of numbers till he finally had Frank on the line.

"Thank God," Beryl said.

*Chapter 43*

Beryl and the Kruck-Boulbrias waited for Frank in the shelter of the blue spruce tree. The rain let up and they were soon able to move about. They didn't talk much. Beryl didn't want to tell them anything, despite their kindness. And they weren't nosy. They made do with the sudden rainstorm, the weather.

Frank was there in fifteen minutes. Mort introduced Ariadne. And Beryl showed Frank what she had found. When he saw what he was dealing with he made a couple of calls, using Mort's phone.

"I guess we'll head on back to school if you don't need us for anything," Mort said, looking at his watch. "We both have classes in a few minutes."

"Yes. Go ahead. By all means," Frank said. "It was good to meet you, Ariadne, even under these bizarre circumstances. I'm sure we'll meet again."

"Are you going to be all right, Beryl?" Ariadne asked. "You should get out of those wet clothes."

Beryl looked down at Stan's gigantic postal shirt. She felt it warranted an explanation, but it seemed too hard. She looked at her neighbour in her fashionable walking clothes.

Ariadne smiled. "Anyway, let us know if we can be of any help. We're off now."

"Thank you both so very much for being here," Beryl said. "And for being so kind."

"No problem," Mort said. He smiled too and they were gone, walking briskly down the cemetery road back to their classes.

Beryl realized she didn't even know what either of them taught.

"They're my next-door neighbours," she said, "and I don't know them at all."

Frank looked at the grave site. He was gentle with the dogwood as he moved it aside.

"Hortense Frouten Keller." He looked at Beryl. "This is the grave of the woman in the Pilot Mound newspaper, isn't it?"

"Yes."

"Oh, God."

"What?"

"It didn't say Keller in the newspaper, did it? It just said, Frouten."

"No. You're right. It did in the *Free Press* though. I went to the library after work and looked it up. It said Hortense Frouten Keller, like it does on the gravestone."

"Oh, my God." The colour had drained from Frank's face. He noticed then that Beryl was still shivering. "I think I have a blanket in the car," he said. "Let me get it for you to throw around your shoulders."

"No, honestly, I'm fine. It's starting to heat up again. Thanks, though."

"Okay. I just have to wait till a forensics guy gets here and then we can go. Tell me everything, Beryl."

She sat down on a flat granite gravestone and told Frank about how the man who helped her in the park was not who he said he was.

"Who did he say he was?" Frank asked.

"Dr. Joe Paine. You know, the famous veterinarian?"

"Jesus Christ," Frank said.

"What?"

"That's not who he told us he was."

"Are you sure?"

"Yes, I'm sure. I would have remembered if the witness had been Dr. Paine. That's who we take Doris and Hugh to. And I read his column all the time. *Doggie Dog Days*, it's called."

"Yeah, I know," Beryl said. "Well…who did he tell you guys that he was?"

"Joe Keller."

"Joe Keller?" Beryl's temples prickled.

"Joe Keller." Frank looked again at the sinister collection of items and the simple marker on the grave: Hortense Frouten Keller.

"Dear God," he said. "We've found him." He corrected himself. "You found him, Beryl."

He looked at her in her damp clothes. "What brought you here? What brought you to this grave?"

Beryl hugged her knees. The sun was coming out. She was glad of her wetness. It would keep her cool.

"It said in the *Free Press* that this was where she was buried and I…I just knew there was something about her. I didn't know that I would find anything here, but I sure did, didn't I?"

"Yup. You sure did."

"So, you saw her obituary in the *Sentinel* then?" Beryl went on. "Didn't it seem odd to you at all? Cold, kind of?"

"Yes. I did see it and yes, it did seem off somehow, but…God, I'm sorry, Beryl," Frank said. "I've been so… And I had to go to that stupid conference. I should have given it a miss. I had to give a paper at it. That's the only reason I went. I should have given it to someone else to read. Stupid fucking paper. Sorry."

"It's okay, Frank."

"That was some hunch, Beryl. Have you ever thought about joining the police?"

She smiled. "No. I hear there's lots of paperwork. I hate paperwork.

"I was really just putting in time till you got back," she said, "and I could tell you about the man who's not Joe Paine." She squinted up at Frank. "He's a murderer, isn't he? For some twisted reason, probably connected to this long dead Hortense Frouten

Keller, he's killing tall thin women. I wonder if Hortense was tall and thin."

"We have to find him," Frank said. "I wouldn't be at all surprised if he's at the address we have for him. He's probably not even hiding. God, I feel so stupid."

"That's quite an assumption isn't it, that he's not hiding? That he's that sure of himself? He didn't seem like that to me," Beryl said. "He seemed more sad and scared."

She thought then of Joe's willingness to give her his phone number, which she never dialled. That carelessness. If she'd had "Call Display" she could have discovered his real name that way any time he called. Of course, that could be easily blocked. If he cared at all.

"Maybe he's some of each," Frank said. "Sure of himself and sad and scared. Maybe he's a multiple personality-type guy. I mean, for one thing, he probably dressed up in women's clothes to do that stuff in your yard. If Mrs. Frobisher is to be believed, and I think she is. This guy is wa-ay gone."

"So you figure that was him too?" Beryl asked.

"Yes. Don't you?"

"Yeah. And Herm's geraniums." She gestured toward the dead flowers. "That was him. This was the first summer she put them outside. It was my idea. I don't think she'll be doing that again."

Frank sat down beside Beryl on another flat stone; they sat atop a husband and wife who had died within the same year: 1927.

Beryl told him about Stan's part in all of it, his discovery of Rollo alive and well in the waiting room of the animal hospital. And how one thing led to another.

"My God, this psycho killer was in my house," she said. "And in Clive's house too."

A man and a woman from the police department arrived and Frank showed them the area to be dealt with.

"Is that eyes?" the policeman asked, pointing to the jar.

"It's an eye," Frank said. "Just the one."

He led Beryl to his car and settled her in the front seat.

"I'm making your car seat all wet," she said.

"Don't worry. Lots worse things have happened to it than that."

"Hermione has disappeared," Beryl said, as they travelled the bleak route from the graveyard back towards downtown.

"No. No, she hasn't," Frank said. "I forgot to mention, she left a message for me."

"For you?"

"Yeah. She called you but you weren't home, or at least didn't answer the phone, and she didn't want to leave a message. She thought that whoever this lunatic is might have the wherewithal to access your phone messages and she didn't want him listening to her, figuring out she was going somewhere."

"Good. Good for Herm. She's quite a bit smarter than me. Where is she?"

"She's safe in the country with some friends of hers out near Tyndall. She didn't leave their name or address or anything, which is fine. She's safe. I do have a phone number for her."

"Good."

"Yeah."

"Okay," Frank said, as he turned onto Logan Avenue. "Let me get this straight. The guy who helped you in St. Vital Park told you that his name was Joe Paine. And that he was a veterinarian."

"Yes."

"He told the police that his name was Joe Keller and that he was a part-time janitor at one of the Catholic schools in St. Boniface, which checked out. So it looks as though it was only you he was trying to trick," Frank said. "I wonder why."

"Maybe he was trying to impress me," Beryl said.

Frank smiled.

"What?"

"Nothing," Frank said. "You're probably right.

"Okay," he continued. "So yesterday you came face to face with Dr. Joe Paine and confirmed what your friend Stan had led you to suspect—that the guy who helped you in the park was not Joe Paine, much-loved veterinarian, author of *Doggie Dog Days*."

"Right."

"Creepy."

"Yes."

"Why didn't you phone the police?"

"I tried quite hard to get hold of you."

"Yeah. Sorry."

"I even left a message with your daughter, Sadie."

"You did?"

"Yeah. She said you might be phoning home."

"I did and she didn't say anything about you having called."

"That's okay. She probably just forgot."

"No, it's not okay."

"Yes, it is, Frank. Please don't yell at her on my account. She was very helpful."

"Still…it was really important."

"Frank, there was no way in the world for her to know how important it was. I probably didn't even say it was important. Promise me you won't yell at Sadie."

"Yes, all right."

"I tried to get the last name of the pretend veterinarian out of Sergeant Christie," Beryl said, "but he wouldn't tell me."

"Prick."

"Yeah."

"And Frank?" Beryl sighed. "It seemed so complicated, you know, all the stuff about flowers and furnace pegs and everything, I thought I'd just wait for you."

"You could have just mentioned that the guy who helped you in the park wasn't who he said he was."

"Yeah, I guess."

"Okay. Never mind. So. While you're waiting for me to come back, you figure you'll investigate the one thing that you saw in the *Pilot Mound Sentinel* that you found to be a little odd." Frank looked at her. "You have good instincts, Beryl."

"Thanks."

"So in the *Free Press* you find that this Hortense Frouten Keller is buried in Brookside Cemetery. You come out to look at her grave and find all kinds of evidence pointing to the guy who killed Beatrice Fontaine and Diane Caldwell."

"Yup."

Frank turned off the Norwood Bridge onto Lyndale Drive. They were almost home.

"I wonder what relation Hortense is to Joe," Frank said. "Mother…aunt?"

"I'm thinking aunt," Beryl said. "I don't think she was a mother."

"It would be interesting," said Frank, "if tall thinness is a part of it, like you say, if that is the connection to the dead women. Whew! I hope this Joe Keller is a talker."

Frank saw Beryl into her house and looked around to make sure everything was as it should be.

"You'll keep me posted, won't you?" she asked.

"I'll call you as soon as we pick him up. If we can't find him, I'll come back. Are you sure you're going to be okay here?"

"Yup. I'm going to lock the doors and wait for your call."

"I think I'm going to get someone over here to sit outside till we get him. Can I use your phone?"

"Yeah. Thanks, Frank. That's a good idea. If you're going to do that, I'll feel safe enough to have a bath and a sandwich."

"Good. Oh. I talked to Katy in the VSU, the gal who's keeping an eye on the boys who found Diane Caldwell."

"Oh yeah. And?"

"Well, neither the boys nor their parents or guardians or whatever have mentioned anything strange going on at their homes. Two of the young fellas have started crawling in with their mums at night, though. Poor little guys."

"Okay. Thanks, Frank. Maybe it doesn't matter now."

"Probably not."

When he left, Beryl locked the door behind him and waited till a uniformed cop pulled up and stationed himself at the curb. Then she poured a tub full of hot water and magnolia-scented bubbles.

## Chapter 44

The doorbell rang an hour later as Beryl was smoothing lotion onto her legs. She looked out the kitchen window and saw the Poulin's truck parked in the lane.

"Yes?" she called through the back door, pulling her terry cloth robe tightly around her.

"Poulin's! For the house next door? I was told to pick up the key here?"

"Could you please step back so I can see you out of the kitchen window?" Beryl shouted.

What she saw when she peered outside was a sturdily built young man, not more than twenty-two, looking up at her. Beside him stood the uniformed cop who gave her a thumbs-up gesture with both hands.

She opened the door to the young exterminator and gave him Clive's key.

"Sorry," she said. "There's been some trouble."

"That's okay, ma'am," he said.

Beryl put on a sleeveless dress, ivory coloured, and then threw a peach tee shirt on over top after catching a glimpse of her arms in the bathroom mirror. She didn't like the look of them.

The phone rang and she picked it up.

"We got him," Frank said.

Beryl sat down where she stood in the middle of her living room floor and began to shake.

"Are you there, Beryl?"

"Yeah, I'm here," she whispered.

"Are you okay?"

"Yeah."

She hauled herself up onto the couch and lay down. Jude and Dusty joined her there, sitting on her chest with their faces as close to hers as she would allow.

Frank came over within the hour. They sat down at the kitchen table.

"He lives on Taché, at the river end," Frank said, "in a house left to him by his aunt, Hortense Frouten Keller.

"You know what he said when he opened the door to us?"

"What?"

"'It's about time.' That's what he said. As though we were a bunch of idiots. I acted gruff, but I sure felt stupid. You solved this for us, Beryl."

"Yeah, I guess I kind of did, didn't I? With Stan's help. And Clive's. And Herm's. And Rachel's. And yours. You believed me when I told you about the crazy goings-on around here. That was really important, Frank." Beryl's eyes filled up.

"Yes, I did that, I guess," Frank said. "I feel like that's about all I did."

Beryl got up to turn the air conditioning off. It was cold in her house. She splashed cool water on her face and pressed a small towel against her eyes to absorb the tears. She didn't want to cry in front of Frank again.

"So what was he like, this Joe Keller?" she asked when she came back.

"Well, I guess you know him as well as, if not better, than I do at this point, Beryl. I mean you've had actual conversations with him, haven't you?"

"Yeah...I have. It just seems so bizarre now that I know he

isn't who he said he was. Like, if I saw him now he might not even look the same."

"He looks the same, all right. Just like he did that day in the park. Like a regular thirty-something guy, kind of handsome, even. But with a horror story inside his head. He's a lone wolf if I ever saw one. He can't name anyone as a friend or even an acquaintance.

"He's had this particular janitorial job for a couple of years. And he's also worked as a security guard and as a night watchman in other places, mostly around St. Boniface. In the summer he just works part time at the school, so he's had a lot of time on his hands. With those types of jobs, he'd have time on his hands anyway, wouldn't he, to brood and imagine and plan who knows what?"

"Yeah," said Beryl. "I guess."

"You know what set him off?" Frank continued. "The pots of geraniums at Hermione's place. Having to walk by them every day to get anywhere. They reminded him of his Aunt Hortense who he really hated. She used to grow geraniums. She sounds like a real prize."

"Was she tall and thin?"

"Yeah, tall and thin, with sparse hair. And bossy. Hermione reminded him of her. She was his prey but she was hard to trap. He just hadn't gotten to her yet. He made do with the other women, with her customers, as he bided his time, till he saw his chance with what he thought of as his real trophy."

Beryl shuddered. "Thank God Herm's okay. Does she know about all this yet?"

"Yes. I talked to her on the phone. She's pretty upset, as you can imagine. She's going stay out there with her friends for a few days. She said to say hi; she'll talk to you soon."

"Okay. Good. So Beatrice and Diane were tall and thin and connected to the shop."

"Yes." Frank fiddled with the salt shaker, trying to balance it on its edge in a little pile of salt he had poured out onto the table.

"God," said Beryl. "Tall and thin with a love of geraniums. How arbitrary is that?"

"And bald. Yeah. Pretty arbitrary." The salt shaker tipped over and caused Beryl to jump.

"Beatrice and Diane weren't even bald," she said.

"No. But, like I said, he made do. He followed them. Hermione didn't give him a good opportunity; at least she hadn't yet. He seems to like to kill outdoors. She doesn't jog, or even walk, it seems."

Beryl smiled. "No. She's the opposite of an exercise freak. Jesus. Thank God."

"He said he hadn't even noticed the shop till this summer when all the geraniums appeared outside. He'd been walking by it for years without giving it a second thought."

The salt shaker banged onto the table again.

"For goodness' sake, Frank!" Beryl said and snatched it out of his hand.

"Sorry," Frank said.

The doorbell rang again. It was the Poulin's guy returning the key.

"I laid some traps," he said, "but he's gonna have to get the holes in his house fixed if he wants to stop the problem. The place is in bad shape."

"I'll tell him," Beryl said. "And I'll try and get him to do something. I know it's bad."

"I seen worse," the Poulin's guy said and was on his way.

"Frank?" Beryl asked. She could see he was getting ready to leave.

"Yes?"

"What about the stuff that happened around here? The cat collar and the furnace pegs and everything?"

"Yes. I'm sorry I don't have anything to tell you about that yet. I will, though. I'm going back to see him again. We had to get the worst of it over with first. The killing part. I'm sorry, Beryl. I know how important those other things are to you. To me too, actually."

"It's okay, I understand."

"We do know that he does make a habit of walking in St. Vital Park on Saturday mornings. We had checked that out right at the start, with other regular Saturday morning walkers and joggers. He didn't lie about that. It was sheer coincidence that he was walking by shortly after you discovered Beatrice's body. Or, as he called it, 'sheer luck.' He wasn't there to hurt you.

"And it came to him on the spur of the moment to pretend he was Joe Paine, the veterinarian. He'd heard of him and how well-liked he is. He figured a vet would seem trustworthy to a young woman such as you. As long as you didn't know the real Joe Paine, that is."

"Wow. Yeah, I did trust him at first," Beryl said. "For maybe an hour or two."

"A prostitute was murdered about eighteen months ago," Frank said. "We're thinking there's a good chance she may have been killed by this guy too. It was a strangulation. With a nylon scarf."

"Charise Rondeau," Beryl said.

"Yes."

"Jesus."

"Yes. We'll see."

"And he's lived right here in the neighbourhood all this time," Beryl said. "That's scary."

"Yup, it sure is."

Beryl opened the drawer in her kitchen desk and found Frank's handkerchief lying on top of Beatrice Fontaine. She gave it to him. And the photograph as well. She knew that Frank would take good care of it, keep it out of Sergeant Christie's hands.

Chapter 45

When Frank left, Beryl phoned Dhani at the pharmacy and he came right over. He made toasted tomato sandwiches for them, using local tomatoes, and afterwards they drank a little brandy.

The evening turned cool. They opened the doors and windows and even built a small fire in the stone fireplace. They cozied up side by side on the couch. Beryl had changed into a nightgown.

She explained everything that had happened, including her own knowledge of Hermione's connection to the killer.

Dhani seemed to understand how she hadn't wanted to confide in him about it. It was one too many connections and he acknowledged that he would have freaked.

"I wouldn't have confided in me either," he said, and kissed the top of her head. "Your hair smells good. Like spring."

Understanding that connection helped. The geraniums, the tall, thin, sparse-haired aunt. But Dhani still wanted to talk about the other ones: Beryl being the one to find Beatrice, Beryl knowing Hermione, and Dhani's knowledge of a pharmacist who knew Beatrice.

Beryl didn't think she could stand to think about those other connections. And said so.

"I want to go over to Hermione's place and make it nice for her before she comes back," she said.

"I'll help you," Dhani said. "Let's plant new flowers."

"Ones that aren't geraniums," Beryl said. "I doubt Herm will want to grow geraniums again, ever."

"I think you're right."

"Dhani?"

"Yes?"

"If I have a party will you come to it?"

"Of course! I'll help!"

Beryl laughed and leaned her head against his shoulder. "You're very helpful today."

Dhani breathed in the scent of her hair. They sat quietly for a time.

"Let's have a bath!" Beryl said.

"You've already had one," Dhani said. "I was thinking of asking if I could use the shower."

"Of course you can. But then let's have a big hot bath, the two of us. And lots of bubbles."

"Yes. All right." Dhani didn't seem so sure.

"It'll be great!"

"Yes. Okay."

When Dhani returned from his shower Beryl was asleep on her side covered with an afghan. Dusty and Jude were curled up in the space next to her heart. Dhani adjusted her blanket and sat down in the easy chair with the *Winnipeg Free Press* and another finger or two of brandy.

## Chapter 46

Frank dropped by Beryl's house the next afternoon, Saturday, to fill her in on more details.

"Do you want to be honoured?" Frank asked.

"What do you mean?"

"Well," he said, "sometimes members of the public are honoured for helping the police in some way. You definitely qualify. I'd like to put your name forward for a civilian citation, but I won't if you don't want me to."

"What would happen?"

"Oh, a little ceremony, probably your picture in the paper, maybe on TV, a memento of some kind. A few of the higher-ups would want to shake your hand."

"Could you let me think about this, Frank? I'm inclined to think I'll pass, but I'll let you know for certain in a day or two."

"Sure."

"I kind of figure solving the crimes was the least I could do seeing as it was my fault in the first place."

"What?"

"It was me who convinced Hermione to put her flowers outside."

"Beryl, that's crazy. Have you spoken to Hermione about this?"

"Yeah. She thinks I'm crazy too."

"If you think that way," said Frank, "you could end up blaming yourself for practically everything."

"Yeah."

"Oh, Beryl." Frank sighed. "That's a heavy load, to say nothing of totally nuts."

"Yeah. I think maybe I'll seek help." Beryl gave a little laugh.

Frank agreed that it might be a good idea.

The day remained cool after the drop in temperature the night before. The sky was bright blue. There was the slightest hint of fall in the air. They sat out back in the screened-in porch with the two cats nestled between them on the couch as Frank filled Beryl in on what he had been able to get out of the interrogation of Joe Keller.

It was all Joe: he dressed up like an old woman, like his Auntie Cunt, as he called her; he deadheaded the lobelia; he attached the collar to Beryl's cat; he moved her furnace pegs; he slept in Clive's bed.

And he left behind the *Pilot Mound Sentinal.* That was the one thing that he hadn't intended to do.

He confessed to it all, as well as to the murders of Diane Caldwell and Beatrice Fontaine. No hesitation. It all just poured out of him.

"Auntie Cunt?" Beryl said.

"Yes. I'm afraid so."

They didn't mean to. And they didn't mean anything by it. But they got to laughing, the two of them, long and hard. They laughed till Beryl couldn't remember what it was that set them off and till Mort shouted over from next door, "Everything okay over there, is it?"

And then Frank continued with his details. "According to Joe, his aunt picked the name Keller because of an article she'd read about a deaf, dumb and blind kid. That's how he described it. She'd read it in a magazine. I guess he means Helen Keller. The aunt must have admired her. Joe stutters when he talks about the aunt. And his voice gets high sounding."

Both the dead women had been joggers. Joe had followed them to the parks and killed them there with his aunt's scarves. In broad daylight. It was easy, he said: a piece of cake, a day at the beach, a walk in the park.

The geraniums that died, the ones that weren't smashed, had been invaded by vine weevils. Joe had gone to some trouble and expense to get them.

Beryl wondered why he picked that particular insect. Vine weevils are all females. There is no male of the species. She wondered why she was cursed with remembering so much useless information.

"Why did he do the stuff at my house, Frank? It's more like mischief than anything else. Except the breaking-in part. That's a bigger crime."

"He took an interest in you. He's been following you ever since the day you found Beatrice. That was his first sighting of you."

"Jesus."

"Yeah. Those were his exact words: I took an interest in her. Except he said 'a interest. I took a interest.'"

"So, how about when I saw him at the folk festival and Wally's funeral? Did he know Wally? Is he a fan of folk music?"

"No and no. He was at both places because of you."

"Jesus Christ."

"Yes. But, somehow, I don't think you were in danger, Beryl. I don't think he would have hurt you."

"How do you know?"

"I don't."

A smoky breeze blew through the screen—the result of the first of the stubble burners, perhaps. Dusty sneezed.

"It's funny you used the word mischief when talking about what he did around here," Frank said. "As well as being charged with first degree murder and break and enter, he is being charged with mischief."

"Really?"

"Yes."

"Goodness."

"Yes."

Frank scratched Dusty behind his little brown ears and the cat closed his eyes and purred.

"There's this one room in his house," Frank said. "With all kinds of paraphernalia: straps and chains. Bondage stuff."

"Oh my."

"Yes. Harnesses, latex masks with holes only for noses…"

"Jesus."

"Yes. He used to invite prostitutes to his home. There are bondage videos, little harnesses for genitals, a cage. I think he actually slept in the cage himself sometimes."

"I don't think I'm up to hearing any more right now, Frank." Beryl wrapped her arms around herself.

"Of course. I'm sorry. I should get going, anyway," Frank said. "I promised my kids I'd take them to the Bridge Drive In this afternoon."

"What about the hooker who died?" Beryl asked.

"He's being coy about that," Frank said, "but we'll find a way to prove it if he doesn't confess. I fully expect he will."

He stood up to go. "Beryl?"

"Yes?"

"If it hadn't been the geraniums it would have been something else. He had already killed once; he was primed to do it again. Charise Rondeau deserves to have her killer found. And you've done that. I hope you can get around to feeling good about some parts of this."

"Thanks, Frank."

"So long, then."

"Frank?"

"Yes?"

"If I have a party, will you come?"

"For sure."

# The Party

Beryl has her party on the Saturday night of the Labour Day weekend. She knows she's taking a chance. The weather could do anything, but she has a feeling it'll be okay.

And it is. The day is as hot as mid-July, not a cloud in the sky and just a hint of a breeze. There have been enough cool nights that most of the mosquitoes are dead.

She spends the day sweeping the deck, hosing down her lawn chairs and preparing snacks. Her wooden lanterns are stuck into the grass here and there around the front yard to give the place a festive air. It's the first time she's used them. She'd bought them from Winnipeg Supply during the closing-out sale of its retail store.

Dhani helps her, as he said he would. He places a metal wash tub on a corner of the deck and fills it with ice for beer. He hauls an old table up from the basement, scrubs it down, and shouts out for a tablecloth.

"This will be the bar," he says.

The snacks are things that Beryl won't have to fuss with once the festivities begin. Like vegetables and dip and hot pepper poppers. And she asks each person to bring something. It's going to be great.

Beryl feels perfect the night of her party, as perfect as one of Hermione's haircuts. She wears Dhani's favourite dress, the blue one, and no shoes and no underwear.

The heat from the day lasts into the night. The guests spend the whole time outdoors and no one even needs a sweater.

Rachel Frobisher brings devilled eggs and celery sticks filled with Cheez Whiz.

Frank brings a watermelon and some chocolate chip cookies that his daughter, Emma, made. He doesn't bring his wife.

The Kruck-Boulbrias bring Camembert in puff pastry. It needs to be heated. But they did it already, at their own house, since they live only thirty seconds away.

Beryl chose not to be acknowledged by the police department so Frank honours her at the party. He stands up and makes a short speech and proposes a toast. They all clap and drink and shout, "Speech! Speech!" but Beryl gets away with not making one. It's her party; she can do what she wants.

Her ghetto blaster is set up on the deck with the speakers pointing toward the house, for all the good it will do. She doesn't want to piss off the neighbours, the ones that aren't there. Burton Cummings is singing "Fine State of Affairs" and Stan Socz turns it up loud.

"I love this song," he says.

The neighbours that are there seem to be enjoying themselves.

Clive comes with a long-legged friend, a couple of cans of smoked oysters, a bag of limes, and three bottles of tequila.

"That oughta do us," Hermione says, helping him set up his supplies at the bar. She brought her trusty bottle of Jack Daniel's and a huge bowl of guacamole with corn chips.

Ariadne Kruck-Boulbria gets drunk. So drunk she kisses all the men on the lips and hugs all the women. No one seems to mind, except perhaps Mort.

Raylene passes around the asparagus and cream cheese roll-ups that she made. She also takes it upon herself to pass the other dishes to the people that find a chair and don't leave it, like Rachel.

Roy, the builder who constructed Beryl's deck, arrives, and she sees him talking to Clive. Maybe they're talking about fixing the holes in Clive's house. She's glad she didn't have to involve her neighbour with the police. Clive is oblivious and it suits him.

Frank has a faraway look in his eyes. He looks as if he needs comfort, but Beryl knows she is not the one to provide it.

She watches while Dhani flips burgers on the grill.

"These are ready for anyone who likes them crunchy!" he hollers. He is cooking vegetables in a foil boat.

Beryl suddenly sees Beatrice, the picture of her that is burned into her memory. She shivers at Dhani's side.

He puts his arm around her. "Are you cold?" he asks.

"No," she says, "just...nothing." She slips out of her yard and walks past three houses to Lyndale Drive and approaches her house from the river end of the street. The breeze has picked up a little and for a moment or two she loses herself in the wind in the trees.

"Hi, Beryl." The small voice startles her back to reality.

"Russell! Hello! You took me by surprise."

"You look like you're missing your own party," Russell's dad says and smiles.

"Just taking a breather." Beryl smiles back. "I hope we're not bothering you with the noise."

"Not at all," the dad says. "I like the sound of a party."

"Me too," says Russell.

"Aren't you up kind of late, Russ?" Beryl asks.

"Couldn't sleep."

"Well, why don't you two join us for a drink? You might even know one or two people."

"I can see Clive," Russell says. "Come on, Dad. Let's."

"Well, okay. Maybe just for a few minutes. Thanks. Beryl, is it? I'm Paul Hearne, Russell's dad."

They shake hands and walk toward the party.

The deck is magical in the dark with the flames from the lanterns. The fragile sound of women's laughter sails out on the night air, disappears far above the tree tops.

Beryl feels a small movement at her side. Russell slips his grubby little hand into hers as he and his father accompany her back to the party.

She stands beneath her willow tree and gazes up into its depths. Everywhere she looks she can see new growth. It's decided to have another go at it, even this late in the season.

MEMBER OF SCABRINI MEDIA

Quebec, Canada
2002